LATE WINTER

Michael P. Charlton

CHAPTER 1

I stand in my rusty tub, naked, washing my body with a sponge that is falling apart in my hand, no state-of-the-art eco-friendly shower, just an abandoned bath in the middle of our kitchen. I still wash like I'm living on the streets. I stare out of my ickle-wickle grubby window at the block of flats opposite. Soaking my man tits with freezing cold water and cringing at my flabby flesh while scrubbing. After I've finished having a cheeky wanky-wanky, I plod to get dressed, simply just slipping into a pair of cum-stained black shorts and a ripped T-shirt. The tub is still full of yellow piss and body hair. I sluggishly limp lifelessly to my armchair, falling into my seat and switching on my tracked digital pocket pad.

Everything is very quiet all of a sudden. My only option is to have a cheeky sip of whisky. I have no problem drowning my liver in liquor or shovelling a palm full of scraps into my giant gob. I keep thinking about this dirty brothel, barely left standing, around the corner from what used to be the old bus station. I wonder to myself if I should go there. I get pissed enough from the whisky to be up for that sort of thing. I've got plenty of time to pop across to this brothel. Pay what little digital currency I have left this month for a depraved punishment. I could get one of those tiny European girls to stand on my face in high heels and treat me like a shitty scumbag. I start fantasizing about this five-foot Latvian girl I know who works there. I imagine her spitting into my mouth and calling me a 'land faggot!' Ha, ha! All joking aside, I'm not going through with it. These are but mere fantasies, which are calmly contained and not to be acted upon. Besides, I begrudge paying to be humiliated twice in one week. Humiliation is free. I feel like an aborted baby thrown to the starving wolves. They're ravenous beasts, dying to chow down on a working-class field beast like myself.

"Fresh Meat!"

Said the crowd as they licked their luscious lips at fresh flesh being tossed onto the pile. I lean over and stare like a gormless divvy out of my window, and the streets seem entirely empty. Most of the shops have been boarded up along the high road, with offensive graffiti covering all the buildings and all the wooden boards. A scruffy drunken tramp appears from an alleyway, stumbling across the abandoned streets far below my gaff. He's tall and skinny, shaved on the back and sides but long on top, with rough stubble, a tracksuit, and trainers. Singing and dancing, clicking his heels, like in one of those old ancient museum films. I feel jealous of the fella. Maybe I'd buy some more booze and join him. Suddenly, a woman, young, short, milky skin, slim, attractive, shoulder-length brown hair up in a bun, comes running up behind him. She's gorgeous. Tarted up like a whore. If I didn't just toss myself off, she would have given me a hard-on. That's one thing I'm proud of about my hideous body. The size of my meat. It's safe to say I've got a proper thick hog.

The two street dwellers begin to argue. I'm not sure what about. I'm too high up to hear a word. The pissed-up bum puts his booze on the ground. Then, out of nowhere, he smashes this bird right in the side of her face, knocking her straight to the ground. I take a step back from the window and cringe. I don't want anybody to see me. I watch the man kick the woman straight in the head from about two inches away. I think she's unconscious? He screams in her face! I feel sorry for her, but I'm too high up to hear what he's saying. This poor girl is undoubtedly dead? The trampy alchy laughs, picks up his booze, sings, downs his drink, and throws the bottle across the street toward the boarded-up shops. The woman lies on her back, not moving even slightly. I think about calling for help, but it's too late. She's probably better off dead. Street tarts don't usually live long.

I put my head in my hands and feel things I haven't felt in a long time. I want to help this woman. Nobody else will help her. We would all lie to say we care about anything outside ourselves. I put on my tatty trainers, grab the rusty key from the floor tiles and go to dash down to help.

Lass comes crashing into the flat. She scrambles around the room like a rat, scratching and nibbling through her little green bag. Then, she quickly dashes from one end of the room to the other like a cat with a firework up its ass.

"What happened?"

"I think somebody recognised me."

"Who recognised you?"

"Don't know."

"You don't know?"

"I was followed."

"You were followed?"

"Yep."

Lass shrugs at me like I'm some kind of street scrounger. Like I'm the alleyway alchy or a dangerous cri-cringle-brekk dealer. What does she mean she doesn't know who recognised her? My bonce starts to overflow with worry and anxiety. Just as my dark thoughts and fantasies began to calm down. She knows exactly how to make my nerves flicker and jitter. But her beauty keeps me quiet. This is the most frantic I've seen lovely Lass as her long, slender limbs fly around the flat. She never usually rambles on like this. How can I keep it together if her marbles have fallen out of her ass?

"Followed by who?"

"Some bloke."

"A bloke?"

"Yes! You worthless cretin. Are you just going to keep repeating what I say?"

"Calm down."

"Where's the razor?"

Lass holds the bag high above her head and empties all of her junk onto the floor. She drops onto her knees and throws all the pointless crap behind her.

She scurries about like a lunatic and has the cheek to snatch my bag. I need to get her to calm down, so I slowly move closer and get her to take deep breaths.

"Just calm down, babe. Deep breaths, deep breaths, deep breaths."

"Get away from me! You oxygen thief."

"Why do you need the razor?"

"I need to shave all of my fucking hair off!"

"Why? Don't be such a silly girl. Don't be such a..."

Go on. Say it. I'm going to say it. She deserves to hear it. It's for own her own good. She needs to know what she is.

"Don't be a stupid bitch."

I usually only call her a bitch when she's tonguing my balls and trying to ram a loaf of bread up my tight boy-pussy hole. We're into that kinky stuff. Some call it kinky. I call it true love, she calls me daddy, and I call her a bitch. Once, she rubbed a thick dump on my chest with her feet. But that didn't quite go as planned.

"If somebody's worked out who I am, they're going to be looking for me, a girl with brown hair, but If I didn't have brown hair, then there's no one to look for. We can't have people looking for us. If anybody finds out where we live, then we're screwed."

She just ignores me. I should have seen that one coming a mile off. Lass finds the razor blade in my bag. That was meant to be for defensive purposes. I thought I'd hidden it away? Her irrationality is really starting to annoy me. It's a good job I love her. Lass throws off her black jacket and leans back into my armchair with the defensive razor in hand. She's even more beautiful in the flesh. Her nipples poking through her disgustingly dirty top. Even while covered in sweat, she looks decent. I'm just a fat lump in shorts and a T-shirt, but Lass's features are on a new level.

"Here we go! We're cooking with gas now!"

Lass proudly holds my razor blade up to the minimal light blazing through a crack in the grimy window. The silver shines like a precious treasure.

"Have you gone mad?"

"I need you to help me shave it all off."

"You've actually lost the plot."

I slowly breeze across the room, away from her madness. I've risked everything for her, and she insists on speaking to me like utter crap.

"Stop giving me shit, be useful for once."

"Useful? How's this for useful? You're a fucking moron."

Am I giving her shit? From my point of view, this isn't what shit looks like. She runs the blade over her head and attempts to shave it. She's going to end up slashing her skull.

"It's not working!"

"Of course it's not working. It's not for your head."

"I need to be bald."

"You need to calm yourself."

Lass starts limping around the room like a wounded soldier, giggling and trying to cut her luscious locks.

"Put the blade down, please?"

She stops and looks directly at me with my razor in her left hand. I'm practically on my hands and knees, begging for her to put it down.

"Let's just talk this through, babe. Alright?"

Lass tip-toes in circles as she gives it some thought.

"Alright, let's talk."

"Right, now, hand over the razor. Give it!"

Jesus, that was a lot of work. But I guess that's what we get for letting each other go outside alone. Finally, she reluctantly hands back my razor blade. She takes a few deep and much-needed breaths. Hands-on hips, heart panting, walking from wall to wall.

"Calm down, yeah?"

"Yep."

Lass nods, and shrugs like she doesn't give a crap about her ridiculous performance. It was a hilarious and violent stand-up show for murderers, abusers, drug dealers, and alchys. I tick all those boxes, so it should have suited me to a tee. But it's hard to enjoy torture when somebody you love does it to themselves.

"This bloke, this man, you didn't know him?"

"No."

"But you think that he knew you?"

"Yep."

"You're para again."

"I'm not para. You're being para!"

Here we go. Another debate over who is more paranoid. Considering my circumstances, with everything I've been accused of, I have more of an excuse to be paranoid about our location. My mind drifts into obscurity once again.

Is that bird outside still there? I slowly creep over to the gap in our boarded-up window to check if she is. Thankfully, I look out with one eye and can't see anything. So either she managed to get herself up, or somebody else helped her. I turn back around toward Lass.

"What did this guy look like then?"

"He was massive, at least six-foot-three, six-four, maybe even six-five, covered in tattoos, giant hands, couldn't work out if he was ripped or just fat, he had tits, a bit like you."

Yet another fat joke. How very amusing. I wonder how many more of these I can take before I just piss all over her sleeping bag.

"This bloke, man, person, what did he do?"

"I was walking around the corner, having a scout about. I'm near where the old station used to be. I see all those cameras pointing at me, at least six or seven. I look up, and my face is blown up in black and white on one of Monsieur's - long live the great Monsieur! - outdoor screens."

"You got caught?"

"Stop jumping the gun, I'm telling you."

"Go on then."

Lass's gestures are big and wide as she fully gets going. She acts like a sadistic cartoon who is singing a devilish song for all of her underground tribe. I stand

and watch like an entertained little sprog during story hour.

"I get out of the way of these cameras and dash down an alley where they can't see me, the one with the really long path. I get a bit of the nervous shakes about me, and realise I can't be getting arrested. Not after, well, you know? Everything that we've done."

"Yep."

"I bail down an alley, and this fat cunt follows me, follows me down the path, down the street, through the park."

"Why didn't you run?"

"I was running."

"How was he still behind you?"

"Because he was running too."

"Did he follow you back here? You retarded idiot. I knew you'd ruin this for us."

"Will you calm down, fat boy? I didn't lead him back here."

"Far enough to spot where you were going. He probably knows where we live. Probably knows who I am, who you are."

"I lost him a few streets back."

"Where did you lose him?"

"At least five minutes away."

"Are you sure he doesn't know where we are?"

"Positive."

He's probably one of those trampy-wamps. The homeless have set up their tents along the old high road. A new community of streetwalkers, like a drug-infested zoo. We both have to watch ourselves very closely. I can tell she isn't sure about what's happened. I can hear her voice and see she hasn't got a bloody clue behind her eyes. I've been able to tell the uncertainty of Lass since we were both kids. I doubt there even was a man who chased her. Maybe it's all just a load of crap. I start to walk around the flat as she quietly stands there. We get to the point where I'm almost circling Lass like a great white shark.

"What was all of that bollocks about shaving your hair?"

"Stop any more people recognising me. Come on, keep up."

"Mistaken identity by the sounds of it."

"You reckon?"

"Maybe."

"Hopefully, that's the last of it."

Lass is undoubtedly lying. I can tell when she's fibbing. I've been able to spot all of the signs since we were about four or five. The funny thing is I would genuinely do anything for Lass. Maybe I should offer to kill him? As a joke, try to make her laugh and see how she might react. Instead, Lass stares blankly at me. She doesn't move, say a word or even blink. Just deadly silent as she scowls at me. Why am I being scowled at?

Her mood is affecting my mood. I'm not the one lying to her.

I can hear alarms in the background. She proudly leans back and grins. Lass turns and walks to my armchair. She silently sits back down, going onto her digital pocket pad. I rub my stubble with both hands as Lass breezes through her pad. Somehow, I'm the one who has taken all of the blame for her craziness. Lass doesn't seem arsed. She's more concerned with her electronic escape route. I'll just keep my giant gob shut from now on.

The night is upon us. It's pitch black outside, and Lass is deep into her digital world. Deep down in my bloated belly, I get this annoying rising sensation, followed by an annoying feeling of déjà vu. I've got a giant lump in my throat like I'm about to cough up a thick, gooey river of phlegm. I stare at myself in the window. Looking back at me is this disgusting, short, stubby, chubby baby boy. I decide to bite down on my bottom lip until it bleeds. Choosing pain over humiliation. The blood oozes onto my thick lower lip. It dribbles down my hairy mush and onto my round double chin. The blood doesn't look real. Maybe there's something about self-inflicted blood that makes it not look natural in comparison? The sharp and sensitive pain gives me these violent, jerking impulses.

Lass lifts herself from my armchair, and we stare at each other. Little butterflies. She leaves her digital pocket pad and strolls over to me. We look into each other's eyes. Her beautiful blue blinkers sparkle and twinkle. We share a peaceful and intimate moment, a moment that only pops up every so often, if at all. This moment of connection between myself and Lass makes everything worthwhile. I'd go through it all again for this one moment. This moment of true love, romantic destiny, and incidental fellowship. All of it. I'd happily stand here and tell her that I loved her over and over and over again. But saying it more than once makes her uncomfortable. It makes her cringe to hear it more than once. I've always got to lead the way.

We move to each other, and I put my sausage fingers down her knick-knacks, going to touch her puss-puss. I remember the first time I ever saw it. We were both six years old, and it was all neatly tucked away. She hadn't got any hair down there yet, but it was still fun for us both. Lass quickly jumps back. She leaps to the other corner of the room, and I give her space to check herself before going over.

"I think I might be coming on."

Lass pulls her hand from her pants. It's covered in lumpy period blood from the tip of her fingers to the bottom of her wrist. I step back as a reddish paint substance entirely engrosses her palms. I see it dripping over her wrists like overdone jam. In between her fingers, stuck underneath her nails, beginning to flow down her arms and take over the entirety of her body. She turns into a period monster, screeching for help.

"I need something to stick up there."

Lass squirms to the hallway. I can hear her checking to see if we have anything to ram up to soak up the mess. Grossed out by all of this, I return to my armchair. I feel absolutely shattered. As soon as I relax and my eyes close, Lass trails back in, wiping all of the period juices from her mittens.

"You're definitely on your period?"

"Looks like it. Before I start pissing blood, will you help me fill my hole or what?" "Urgh! Rank."

"Don't be such a little tart."

"I'm not having sex on your period. I'm not gay."

"Because you don't like blood. I've heard it all before."

"Yeah."

"Only a bit of red liquid. If you were a real man, you'd get amongst it. I can't remember the last time you got down there and gave me a good seeing too. Scared of periods."

"It's not about the period. It's about the blood."

"How do you think I feel having to go through it every month?"

"But you're used to it."

"Doesn't get any easier."

"I'll never get used to blood."

"We're not getting into another period debate."

I nod and grunt. My eyes feel like piss holes in the snow, bags hanging halfway down my face, just about managing to look at Lass. I need a little drinky-wink. I go over to my half-packed bag, pull out a fresh bottle of whisky, and swig from it. This has been in here quite a while for such an occasion. I deserve a swig. I neck the whisky straight from the bottle and creep around the flat with an incessant ringing in my ears. The drinky-wink really starts to wake me up.

"Want a sip?"

"Thanks."

I sheepishly stand very stiff and awkwardly shuffle from one leg to another. Finally, me and Lass meet halfway across the room and embrace, having a big cuddle.

"No more arguing?"

"Agreed."

"Promise?"

"Pinkie promise."

"That's a proper fucking promise."

"You're cute."

"You're cuter."

"You're funny."

"You're funnier."

We kiss and hug as passionately as possible and have a cheeky drink. Lass takes a couple of big swigs, and then so do I. There's not much left. We hold each other's hands and playfully swing our arms like when we were kids.

"I love you."

"I love you too."

We have a peaceful moment together.

I slump over to our window. Lass seems amused as she watches me curiously. She sits with her legs crossed on the floor. It's gotten busier below as all the creatures come out at night.

"Teleport Boy's trying to buy."

"But he brought last night?"

"I know, clearly, he's sniffed it all."

"How could he sniff all of that in one night?"

"The magic of cri-cringle-brekk."

"Freaks."

"Yep."

"How's he looking?"

"Pasty. I swear his head's getting bigger."

"Is he still wearing that eye patch?"

"Yep."

"Teleport Boy's a legend."

"I reckon he's a civil war vet."

"Suffers from PTSD?"

"Pill addict more like."

"Let me see!"

Me and Lass switch places. Lass is now staring out of the little hole, and I watch her from the crusty yellow floor like a pair of tipsy toddlers. My medium-sized bottle of whisky is also gone. We've managed to quickly gulp it down in a few swigs.

"What can you see?"

"Teleport Boy's gone."

"Teleported back into the future?"

"Nah."

"Shame."

I wish I could teleport back and forth from past to future. Getting to use all of the state-of-the-art, highly functioning devices. About the only thing around here that is working. No wonder everybody is leaving. Most of the shops can barely stay open or even allowed to stay running. Maybe by the end of next month, I'll have sunk so low that I'll be sucking off some old smackhead for an online score. Electronic smack straight into my purple veins. Everything left standing in this torn-apart city is digital. That which doesn't fit within the new electronic and technological era simply goes out of business. Sure, there are a few exceptions, where you can still get fatty foods, booze, and a suck, but most day-to-day services are significantly reduced. You better have your digital passcode! Even for a quick suck, you still have to put your dick through a tiny (I mean huge!) databased type hole in the wall.

"Oh shit! Guess what?"

"What?"

"Bog Roll's out."

"Whey! Bog Roll."

"She looks sad."

"I would be if I looked like that."

"Don't be mean."

"I'm just saying, three times she's had dirty bog roll on her shoe."

"I know, but she's clearly not well."

"Clearly not cleaning her ass properly either."

"She's got a cute dog, though."

"Baby Eater."

"Do you think?"

"One hundred percent."

"You think her dog eats babies?"

"Yep."

"What's wrong with Bog Roll?"

"Divorced."

"Kids?'

"Not a chance."

"Single?"

"Definitely."

"Just her and the dog."

"Baby Eater!"

Lass leaves the window and returns to the floor. We both sit crossed-legged and gaze at each other with huge grins. Lass unwraps some cri-cringle-brekk. She chops a line on the floor with my razor blade, halves it, and we sniff it straight from the ground. The high hits us both instantly! Lass doesn't reply. She slides off me, stands up, and slowly floats off. I start tripping and try to get my bearings. The shock keeps you from thinking clearly. Sporadic episodes of screeching static, fuzziness like shock waves on one of those massive screens. I'm too distracted to really care. My mind wanders off into fantasy. Reality and magic merge into one. I disappear out of the room as the trip truly takes hold.

Once upon a time, we would all meet around the sun rising outside the fruit market after the big cleanup. Those unfortunate enough to be demanded a dark shift would be left notes written on the market walls. Bitter and resentful, we would kick and spit at the dirt and fucking filth left behind by the chorus of Monsieur - long live the great Monsieur! The shitty city chorus would cackle and sing as they would make the stalls as mucky as possible for a cleanup. Those put on command for an all-eventful dark shift would even have brown slop and green liquids to scrape off the streets ready for the fruit markets.

The chorus would make our pickups miserable with harassment and assaults. Everybody else got a completely free pass. They stuck up their clackers and positions of privilege to bypass the humiliations of real life onto the workers of the land. We spent long days and dark nights, depending on our assigned schedules, forced to do unpaid labour along the streets and greenery of the grounds. Sometimes this labour even got destroyed and burnt to a crisp. Then, a large chorus or a mob would appear seemingly out of nowhere. They would chuck rotten tommies and scabby apples at our noggins, mock us, laugh at us, cackle like witches, and poke us with sticks. They would scream and spit abuse at us and angrily accuse us of being the ones who were harming them.

We were forced to rebuild and start again, strictly for their entertainment. Having to earn our scran to munch and wet our lips with chloride. The crew was given breaks when we couldn't stand up or breathe any longer. After our legs had given way and our lungs had nipped to sleep for a short break. Monsieur - long live the great Monsieur! - had a specific aim in mind, which still, to this day, is one of his primary goals. That is, to turn what's left of our land into a destructive mess like his city. He hates that which still stands.

As the orange sun came up for its third turning, in the distance of the pink sky, I would slump my clogs along the streets of the land after a dreary and devastatingly long pick up. I'd pass the crumbled ruins and torn-apart houses, going from the blackened paths onto the green grass. Having to stomp through mud and shit as I left the streets and made it back onto the rough and rocky roads. After a few miles of stumbling along, I'd return to the small village centre where I could snooze. I usually hurried to return to my wooden shack where I would sleep.

The trek would be so long that I'd start to get the uncomfortable urge to piss my pants. Alone and hungry. So very bastard hungry. I would return to the roads and head for my shit shack. I returned to my hole, poured some mucky, stinky water on my face, and dressed in my usual relaxed attire. I stumbled to the door, pushed it open, and vomited inside. I'd slam the door shut behind me and stare outside. Gazing at the rain in silence and feeling like a worthless piece of shit. I needed freedom from the chorus enslavement.

I'm out of the trip and back in the flat. I go to check on Lass and try to see if she's having a bad trip. If she's fleeing like I am. I start to fall across the room. Trying not to drop back down onto the yuck-yuck floor. I sway from left to right. Lass looks as though she might cry. She must definitely be having a bad trip. Maybe another line would balance her out? Lass's head swells to three times its size. Purple veins burst from her forehead, pulsing with two beats per second. I try to control my breath and say nothing. I only care that Lass's head looks like a talking moon. I'm sat on this big, long, thick dick as a chair. I keep my mush closed and watch moon girl from my dick chair. I leave Lass to it and start sluggishly floating around, almost falling over my clown shoes. My mind evaporating into thin air. I collapse and sit hunched over, hugging my knees to my chest in the cold and lonely corner of the flat. I start to get a queasy feeling in the pit of my stomach. Like I'm about to be sick. I don't say a word as I wait for it to pass. The queasy sensation turns into hyper déjà vu. The worst I've ever had! I know nothing of my world and surroundings.

HAAAWWWHHH!!!

HAAAWWWHHH!!

HAAAWWWHHH!

CHAPTER 2

I'm starting to think clearly. I can hear the sound of my own voice again. I can think. Still unable to get my speech back. I can't speak. Not a single word. I can only make baby noises and farmyard grunts.

I look around the room and literally can't remember a thing. I've not a clue what's happened to me. Where am I? What the hell is happening to me? I wriggle around in my bed, broken springs poking into my back and pillows as hard as rocks. I turn onto my left side to give my back a break from the pain. But it's no use. This worn, tattered mattress makes me want to violently roll out of bed. Even if I do drop onto the solid floor. It looks like some kind of shitty-hospital place. It smells, well, God knows what that disgusting smell is. Baby sick? Dog crap? Maybe I should try to lick the bed and see if it has that weird hospital taste. I can't take this any longer. I try my best to stand up, twisting onto my front, twirling my legs to the left side, lowering my legs and feet onto the hard ground, then using my hands to push against the bed and force myself onto my feet. I just about manage to stand up.

I look down, and I'm dressed in some kind of ridiculous blue hospital robe thingy, which looks like a dress. At least I can hear my own voice again. That's something. I put my head in my hands and feel a pain on the top of my head. I brush the centre of my noggin and feel a sharp shooting shock. Argh! I gently stroke with one finger what feels like a deep cut with stitches. Fuck me sideways. Have I had my bonce stitched up? I think I've banged my head. That would make sense. I look around and am so confused. Where is this? It looks like a frigging hospital. My body feels so stiff, and staring at these bright white walls is starting to make me feel dizzy.

I was mumbling and stuttering for way too long. I'm incredibly grateful to be able to hear my own words and move my limbs. Before I have time to properly collect my thoughts and work out what the hell is going on, I hear a loud knock.

Bang!

A loud knock on the door across the room. My heart starts to beat really fast. Bum, bum, bum, bum. My pulse is so hard it feels like it's going to burst out of my neck.

Bang!

Another knock.

"Come to the door."

I limp to the other end of the room, farthest away from the door, near a broken wooden chair with a leg missing. I try to crouch and hide, but the pain in my back is too much.

Bang!

"Let us in, please, sir."

I'm going to have to bite the bullet. I slowly limp to the door, nearly falling over. I twist the metal lock and open it.

"Would you like to come with us, sir?"

"Err. Err."

I sheepishly nod like a coward. So much for me biting the bullet. These two guys look like secret agents. Dressed in their black suits, and white shirts, they wouldn't look out of place with a pair of sunglasses. Secret knob heads more like it.

"You need to come with us."

I say nothing. Just nod and agree. No questions. Next, I'm being carted off down a long, narrow hallway. No memories of where I am or how I got here. It fucking stinks too. What is that bloody smell? Who are these twats, and where the hell are they taking me?

I'm roughly dumped into what can only be described as an interrogation room. Argh! Calm down. That was too hard. They dump me down into a seat with a table, two empty chairs in front of me, white padded walls, and bright lights. The secret knob heads leave. I'm sitting alone. There are so many cameras in this room! At least six cameras recording me throughout. Two big chunky chub-chubs walk into the room, new men, more muscular and scary bastards. These two look more like bouncers. They've got that tall and overweight look. Couldn't go for a run but could kick your fucking head in. They both sit opposite me. We all stare at each other.

"Do you know why you're here?"

Asks this massive idiotic twat. He doesn't even have the courtesy to call me sir like those other two dick-poles. I shake my head.

"Have you started to remember anything yet?"

The bigger of the two pricks looks like the other's younger brother, with fewer wrinkles on his face. He smiles and tries to scare me. He likes that I can't remember anything. Maybe he wants to bum me? I'm confident that there's a camera looking up my nose to see my nostril hairs. I'd love to make them terrified of me. Watch them cower in the corner as I stand over them, asking them to beg for their lives. Dig their own graves and apologise for all of the damn cameras. I'd shit into a hole in the ground, point a gun at both of their heads and slowly make them eat my sloppy Giuseppe.

"If you can't remember by now, we'll have to book you to see Top Doc."

Top Doc? What Top Doc? Who the hell is Top Doc? I don't know of any Top Doc?

These two losers watch me like a pair of disgusting hawks. The men begin to write on these digital screen thingamajigs. I start to quietly panic but try to keep it inside. They must have made a mistake? This was all just one big mistake. The dickheads lean back and speak to one another. This room is freezing cold. Why is it so cold in here? Making my little nipples hard through the blue gown. I just sit here, shivering and staring at them. The bigger of the two leans over toward me. I'd love to spit right into his eye. He's got a scar just below his right eye. And I've got a big greeny with his name written on it. They look at each other, giggle like little girls, and stare directly through me as though I'm not even here. My jaw slowly drops back down to the table, and it feels like I've stopped breathing. These two shitbags look at me as though I'm guilty of something. I think the grey-haired one fancies me. There isn't an ounce of presumption of innocence behind their gormless, stupid, ugly mugs. The seriousness of the situation stabs me right in the pit of my stomach. I no longer think that they've made a mistake.

I've been sitting in this cramped office for quite some time. And, guess what, I've got my speech back! Finally, after a long wait, I started to be able to form words, then sentences, and now I can have a conversation. I spoke to a nurse who brought me to this office space. One of the late specialist doctors who works on the unit enters and takes his seat opposite me. Roughly sixty years old and equipped with one of those digital screen thingamajigs. Electrical tech seems to be all the range in this cesspit. Top Doc focuses on taking notes while I struggle for mere acknowledgment. I was already incredibly agitated and becoming even more nervous and uncomfortable. My posture feels tense, and I can't stop fidgeting in my seat. After some time, Top Doc finally puts everything down and calmly begins a conversation with me. I'm his first patient of the day. Lucky me, I feel so special.

"Now, you've been referred to the centre for special treatment? It seems to me we still don't know very much about you. At the centre, we try to befriend our patients and make them feel at ease. We like them to feel they can trust us enough to open up about their lives, so we can help and advise them best. Does that sound reasonable to you?"

Top Doc has taken me by surprise here. Rambling on and referring to this as treatment rather than punishment? Why does it feel so much like punishment? What is he talking about, wanting me to trust and feel at ease? I simply just look away, the stupid old fool. I want to make his job more challenging. The daft cunt. I anxiously stare at the white medical ground and refuse to answer Top Doc's questions. I like the idea of giving Top Doc a taste of his own medicine. Shoot me, and I'll shoot you right back.

"Does that sound reasonable to you? It may seem overwhelming to have left your home and stay at the centre, but for many of our long-distance patients, leaving their home was exactly what they needed."

He seems to know more about my life than I do. Left home? Top Doc can only maintain his interaction for a short time. Then, he returns to his digital screen thingamajig. Nervously hiding his weirdly shaped egg head. Making naughty notes about me. I avoid eye contact with him at all costs. Top Doc seems just as awkward as I am, yet I'm meant to be the patient? He continues to take notes in silence before putting his digital screen thingamajig back onto his desk. He takes a couple of deep breaths and annoying sighs.

"Do you know why you've been sent to us?"

He embarrassingly tries to offer me his fake compassion. Let's be honest. There's no such thing as compassion. So I just shake my head and shrug at any of his questions.

“Why don’t you tell me more about why you think you’ve been sent here?”

He’s really starting to get on my tits now. I clench my fists together under the desk, push my tense jaw out and bite my teeth together like a rabid dog looking to chase a violent cat.

“It’s OK. You’re in a perfectly safe environment. Whatever is said in these sessions stays between the two of us. The centre abides by a strict, one hundred percent confidentiality policy.”

Ha! Top Doc continues to show me his fake compassion. There’s no such thing! The fucking lying, ugly tit-head. He places his magical digital thingamajig behind him instead of in front of him. Trying to play tricks on my brain box. I start to doubt myself. Maybe he can fool me. I’m sitting here without anybody to help me.

“What are your feelings about your stay at the centre?”

I don’t even know what centre he’s talking about. Top Doc leans back in his chair, inhales, and sighs loudly. I wonder if he will ever get any information from me during this session. Then, he starts to make me incredibly irritated. I pull at my blue hospital gown and start scratching my legs. I wish I could remember something of worth. As might be expected, yet again, Top Doc obsessively returns to his digital screen thingamajig and begins making notes. I sit, scratch, and shuffle in my cramped chair. After a while, he returns to me with some more questions.

"Well?"

Top Doc picks up exactly where he left off, as though he hadn't just checked out of the conversation for a couple of minutes. Leaving me here to stare at the glowing white ceiling, the cameras, and the lights!

Argh! Screen, scratch, shuffle, talk, what centre? Repeat. Argh! Screen, scratch, shuffle, talk, what centre? Repeat. Argh! Screen, scratch, shuffle, talk, what centre? Repeat. Argh! Screen, scratch, shuffle, talk, what centre? Repeat. Argh! Screen, scratch, shuffle, talk, what centre? Repeat. Argh! Screen, scratch, shuffle, talk, what centre? Repeat. Argh! Screen, scratch, shuffle, talk, what centre? Repeat.

I'm trapped in this mind-numbing cycle of repetition.

Argh! Screen, scratch, shuffle, talk, what centre? Repeat. Argh! Screen, scratch, shuffle, talk, what centre? Repeat. Argh! Screen, scratch, shuffle, talk, what centre? Repeat. Argh! Screen, scratch, shuffle, talk, what centre? Repeat. Argh! Screen, scratch, shuffle, talk, what centre? Repeat. Argh! Screen, scratch, shuffle, talk, what centre? Repeat. Argh! Screen, scratch, shuffle, talk, what centre? Repeat.

"Fuck you!"

I couldn't help myself. I spit out words that were brewing deep within my tum-tum. Some spit leaves my mush and lands on Top Doc's desk. I might spit on him some more. I might jump on the desk and start firing ammunition of spit.

"Excuse me?"

Top Doc glances at me like a museum statue. Maybe he's fallen in love with me? He wants to marry me and adopt some kids? He's waiting for me to speak again. I'm starting to feel like a lost little boy, but I want to be a brave, strong man. Energy drains from my body. I don't know what's going to happen to me.

"Just tell me what I'm fucking doing here!"

I slam my fist onto the table and shoot across the desk as fast as possible. I'm more and more anxious, more and more uncomfortable, more and more self-conscious, more and more raging. I lean halfway across the desk without a flipping clue what to say next. My face is hot, and my eyes are as wide as can be. We both go silent. We both stay silent. I slowly lower myself down and sit back in my chair. Top Doc slowly leans back into his chair. We don't say a word. I can't help noticing eight cameras in the room, two in each corner. Watching and tracking my every move.

"We just want to help you to get better."

"Fine."

I nod my head in agreement. After my outburst, I'm more aware of these bastard cameras watching me, waiting. Top Doc returns to taking notes for what feels like the hundredth time. I stare into space again, deep in thought. Gawping at the ceiling. Top Doc looks up from his screen.

"I promise we'll fix you."

Top Doc attempts to console me from across his desk. Teeny-weeny tears slowly stream down my pale and fragile face. I'm so confused. I feel like a tiny child who has lost his mummy. I exhale and collapse back into my chair, exhausted. I can't keep up any longer. I need somebody to hold me near them.

I put both hands on the top of my head.

"Don't touch it, young man. I just mean it's fresh. But, of course, you want to keep everything in place. You don't want to bleed, do you?"

"Bleed?"

"Yes."

"Urgh! Stop.

"I take it you don't like blood?"

"Sshh! Stop it."

"That's where you had the operation."

"What operation?"

"Yes. Good boy."

"I've had an operation?"

"Just be careful, it's fresh, and your brain will still be getting used to the fitting."

"What the hell are you talking about?"

"It's your surgically fitted brain chip."

The room begins to quickly spin. I beg for it to stop. The scar on the top of my head, starts to hurt.

"You just need to tell me if your scar feels uncomfortable. Otherwise, well, things will continue to worsen for you. Look at what you're doing to yourself, young man. I want to help you, but you need to tell me everything. Everything that you can remember. Everything that's happening, everywhere that you've been. All of it. Stop playing these games with me."

I look down at my thick-hanging mittens to see sticky blood underneath my fingernails. I put them behind my back. My head suddenly drops onto the desk, and I can't look up. Top Doc makes notes. He doesn't even attempt to help me.

He's got all he needs from me, his patient. After a while, I look up from the side of his desk. Forced to stay in a medical centre in the middle of nowhere. They've been putting it in fancy terms, but by the sounds of it, I'm their lab rat.

"Don't try to fight us. So many have tried and failed. The best thing to do is give yourself completely over to the centre. If you will, just comply. If you continue to resist our help, the help I'm trying to give you, then you will, well, you know…Which is it to be?"

"I'm sorry."

I apologise to Top Doc. I'm so done with this. I genuinely apologise for being so difficult. I'm emotionally drained and shattered. I'm ready to fall asleep. Top Doc makes his final notes on his digital screen thingamajig. This is exactly what the bastards in this place wanted all along. Complete control and acquiescence. They've won. They have me in the palm of their goddamn hands.

"When will I be able to leave?"

"The treatment at this centre lasts as long as you want it to."

Top Doc grins, shrugs, and puts down his notes. He's done with me for today.

"I understand."

"Have a think about what I've said. We've got another session booked for you soon. Nurse will be over to collect you in a few minutes. So just take this before you go, please."

Top Doc gives me a massive white pill. I take it from him as Top Doc pours me a paper cup of water. I twist the big white pill to one side, and it says one-thousand-five hundred mg in giant letters. I look up at

Top Doc. He smiles at me encouragingly to take the pill. I stick the massive pill into my gob and drink the water in one gulp. I'm shown the door to leave the office. I waddle around in the centre's halls. I realise what I have to do. As I wait for the nurse, I start to get this weird queasy feeling deep in my stomach. Things seem very strange. Really weird. I feel sick. My scar is banging. I feel like I could shit myself and drop to the floor simultaneously. Reality loses itself, and my five senses start to evaporate. One, after the other, after the other, after the other. I fall to the floor and drop down head first in slow motion.

HAAAWWWHHH!!!

HAAAWWWHHH!!

HAAAWWWHHH!

CHAPTER 3

I'm an overweight little scrounger, sprawled out on my back like a starfish, arms dangling so that my uncut fingernails trail back and forth against the fluffy, soft front room carpet. I'm a trampy degenerate who is willing to sacrifice everything. Waking up stuck to the black leather sofa after a heavy night on the ol' boozy-woozy. Crushed-up and empty cans littered all over the place like rotting autumn leaves. A cheap bottle of warm vodka burns the back of your throat yet tastes fantastic at the same time. I like things that glow. I've completely ruined the entire fresh, cream, pure wool carpet. A colourful rainbow of stains. They look gorgeous as they stain their way across the room.

Sometimes I can't make it up the stairs to the spare cupboard, which I'm allowed to sleep in. I'll often vomit into my hands and wipe the stinky slop up the walls as I slide back down, back into the front room, like a pissed up teeny-tot returning to his naughty step after shitting it's nappy. The small cupboard across the landing from the other two rooms consists of a mattress on the floor that goes from the door to the window. Three blue baskets, each with the handles snapped off, crammed against the damp walls, filled with what little clothing I have left, which always falls onto the mattress. My digital pocket pad is crammed down the side and digging into my ribs, which I'm forced to sign into every morning and night when the red tracing alarm rings throughout the house.

I'm currently staying with Gammy Leg. What started out as a long overdue bonding opportunity for us has become a nightmare. My drinking has become too much for either one of us to bare. I don't see the point in food anymore, only shovelling Gammy Legs greasy leftovers at meal times, whenever I absolutely have to, so that I don't die. Gammy Leg lives on the land, the countryside haven which, until now, has been left alone, somehow surviving the tearing down of everything, unlike the city.

I've been working for Gammy Leg as a farm hand, even though half of the time, I'm hungover and constantly nipping off for a Tommy tank. I've also become addicted to watching cheap homemade sex videos on my pad. Homemade clips of siblings shagging each other senselessly. Mothers and sons, dads and daughters, even humans and animals. It's an addiction that has always, without a doubt, left me with a sense of internal guilt once I've finished. I understand freedom for all, but I could never imagine screwing Chip Fat Mam or a little cocker spaniel dog. I'm usually on my hands and knees on Gammy Legs bathroom floor, forced to wipe up my glowingly white jizz and flush it down the state-of-the-art eco-friendly toilet. To be fair to Gammy Leg, he's kindly allowed me to come work for him, to live with him for the time being on the land. Paid in full via the wild west style of digital currency. Through our tracked and traced digital pocket pads. All introduced and enacted by tech mogul Monsieur - long live the great Monsieur! While I was most desolate, alone, and suicidal, I'd found Gammy Leg to fall back on after all this time.

I stretch out, barely conscious, on the leather sofa from the previous night's solo sesh. My raging uncle Gammy Leg comes thudding down the stairs in tight, laced-up black boots. I can hear his dodgy leg thud and drag behind the rest of his body. Back in the day, he worked in a fish factory. He gutted and prepared fish after being caught so they could be sold and eaten. He ended up getting into an argument with an Arab over the west. Funnily enough, I actually agreed with the Arab. He smashed the Arab in the face, busting his lip wide open. The Arab, not one for taking a beating from a "fat white cunt" grabbed one of the work knives and stabbed him through his thigh. Uncle swaggered away, proud that he had hit an Arab to defend his land. Next thing, he sees blood dripping from his leg. He didn't even know that he had been stabbed!

Gammy Leg storms into the front room and tramples the thick, gunky mud from his boots all over his new cream, pure wool carpet. His six-foot frame, broad shoulders, and large, round Father Christmas belly, covered in purple stretch marks, roughly five stone heavier than me. He towers over his own sofa like a giant inspecting an ant. His unshaven and unbrushed grey beard was left to hang with pride. Dressed in his dark green farmers' work clothes, his black work cap protecting his bald patch from the sunlight, his scraggly beard going into his mush and up his nose. Gammy Leg screams at the top of his husky land-man voice right into my lifeless little face, making my dried-up chops quiver.

"Get your fucking stuff together!"

I leap up onto my feet. Swaying from side to side, hanging out of my arse. I was already having one of my nightmares, so this really scared the shit out of me.

"What? What's happened?"

I'm so dizzy and delirious, trying to make sense of the world. Gammy Leg is furious and barely able to catch his breath after charging like an overweight rhino into the room. Breathing heavily, he's a dragon with smoke puffing out his nose. After taking a few long, hard, deep, meditative breaths, Gammy Leg eventually returns to normality and calms himself down. He's finally able to get his words together. I look at his fucked-up leg and see he's hardly putting any weight onto it.

"I said…"

Gammy Leg clears his throat to really get his point across more clearly. Steam blowing out of his cauliflower ears, he's a boiling hot kettle, gritting his brown stained teeth together. He looks like he wants to eat me. Maybe it will be fun getting digested into Gammy Leg's gutty goo? The gross imbecile hasn't had any food since yesterday. I'm pretty sure that he's ready to chow down.

"I said get your stuff together and do one."

Gammy Leg claps his hands together, making me jump back from shock. My dopey jaw drags along the floor. I rub the crusty gunk out of my watery eyes, like piss holes in the snow. That one never gets old. On a more serious note, I need to find out what's happened. It's probably best to just ask the gross imbecile.

"What's happened, mate?"

I'm still oblivious and need to wake up. Gammy Leg finds my questions hilarious, tilting his head back and letting out a massive roar of laughter like an overweight ogre.

"You're seriously asking me?"

Gammy Leg repeats himself in his thick land accent, perfectly fitting for someone who lives on a farm. How could I possibly ask such a brain-dead question? Am I a retard? Yes. I'd have to agree that I'm a bit of a spacker. I need to make sense of Gammy Leg's madness. So I'll ask another question to the gross imbecile.

"Why do I have to leave, mate?"

I ask this question with profound hesitation. He isn't my mate, but the word works if you need to get something that's out of your reach. I've still not got foggiest as to what's happening. It's too early to think. Thinking is for those who are awake.

The gross imbecile lunges himself at me. Fuck! He grabs me first by the collar, then by the scruff of my neck, and drags my lifeless corpse through the front room, double doors, and outside into the neat and tidy back garden, with his leg dragging behind.

Whop! Whop! Whop!

The cool spring breeze suddenly hits me. I gawp up at the clear blue sky. A sigh of relief as the sun gives me a much-needed boost. Not too hot, but lovely and calming. Gammy Leg throws me down onto the grass. His flowers and plants, which sit at the bottom of the square garden, are all destroyed. I feel so confused and vulnerable. At only five-foot-seven, I stand no chance of fighting against podgy Gam Gam. A man who is perfectly comfortable and relaxed regarding a scrap. He loves a good game of fisty cuffs with whoever is willing to enter the ring.

"What's that, soft boy?"

Soft boy, soft boy, soft boy. He knows I hate it when he calls me that. Gammy Leg aggressively points at me with his stained fingers for an answer.

"Where, mate?"

I play dumb as I tread carefully and try to calm things down. Last night was a heavy sesh. I've been drinking hard for months now. Indulging in this kind of behaviour was nothing new to me. Gammy Leg has never mentioned anything before. He has a few swigs and a couple of lines of cri-cringle-brekk most weekends, just not during the weekday. Maybe Gammy Leg has finally had enough of me? Although I was merely assuming that Gammy Leg's invitation to come live and work on his farm meant that he genuinely understood my depression. That he would perhaps cut me some slack? A frustrated Gammy Leg repeats himself again and again. Slapping his curly and itchy beard with his own penis-shaped fingers. Any respect for Gam Gam melts away.

"What's that? That pile. Down there on the grass."

"I'm not sure."

I shrug a couple of times. I can definitely see where the Arab was coming from. I look around the garden to see if there's a fish knife to hand.

"Of course, you know. It was you who did it, soft boy?"

Jesus-Christ-almighty! Soft boy, again. The gross imbecile is pissed off, and he's pissing me off. The kettle begins to boil within his hard skull. My head is still pounding.

"Come on, soft boy? Answer me."

Gammy Leg clearly thinks I'm lying. Maybe I am a lair. Perhaps we're all liars. I stare at the blue sky and ponder whether I could be a liar. Can we lie and genuinely not know it. Saying that you're not a lair is a lie. Truth is the myth. Lying is the truth.

"Whose shit is that on the grass?"

Gammy Leg slowly begins to calm himself down. The sun and breeze are helping. Cooling and relaxing our gormless faces. I look from left to right at the high, brown fences, considering if I could jump over one of them in the worst-case scenario. I don't think I'd have a chance of escaping at nearly seven feet tall. I assume it's my turd sausage from the rank smell and colour. Three long pieces of shit were all over his crumbled plants. Definitely looks like mine. Smells like one of mine. All are laid neatly alongside each other, like a plate of dippy eggs and brown soldiers.

"It's, err, my shit, mate."

Whether I could remember it or not, I just confessed. I know Gammy Leg wants a confession. This was followed by silence. Silence follows me wherever I go. I may need to get my ears checked out. I can still hear the birds tweeting in the trees. A beautiful, relaxing sound surrounded by magnificent green nature. No wonder, so many posh city pricks are leaving in droves to come live on the land.

Eventually, the beauty and magnificence fade into dust and nothingness.

Gammy Leg leads the way back inside, still stomping about and dragging his thick log of a leg. I remember when shit used to be funny. Not anymore. We're rarely allowed a laugh nowadays. As we return to the front room, I follow him like a naughty schoolboy. Giant, sized fourteen, gunky mud footprints mark the pure wool carpet. We both slowly sit on the soft sofa, eyeing each other like stray alley cats.

"I couldn't, err, I just couldn't get into the house, mate."

Gammy Leg stares at me blankly. Like I'm an idiot who needs to learn sign language. Gammy Leg has gotten his confession out of me. He has dropped his anger levels ever so slightly, a teeny-weeny amount. His heavy, tense, eighteen-stone shoulders have loosened.

"I needed to take a shit, mate."

"When you need to go for a dump, you wait. Yeah? Otherwise, people would just be crapping everywhere. Wouldn't they? You have to respect the land, soft boy."

Soft boy, again! I've told him about that. Gross imbecile. I nod up and down like a dog listening to car music. Far too hungover to snap at being spoken to like a baby. I'm used to it by now. Gammy Leg patronises me daily. He shouts at me like a naughty boy whenever I don't do exactly what he wants. This time is no different. He looks at me with disappointment.

"I mean, who takes a shit in somebody else's garden? You're an animal. That's what you are. A fat and disgusting animal."

I've been called an animal before. Quite a few times, as it goes. The lump in my throat returns once more as my left hand begins to shake, fearing I may break down and cry like a faggot. I try to swallow my prideful lump of emotion. Finally, I manage to steady my left hand, stop it from shaking, and slowly stable my squishy body, so I can contain my dark thoughts in front of Gammy Leg. I can cry later when nobody is looking, maybe while I'm napping down some alleyway and lying in my own piss.

"You should have shat your knickers, soft boy."

Gammy Leg smirks at me, the twat, smirking and enjoying my pain. He loves the power of knowing he can bully me and get away with it. I don't even know what to say to Gammy Leg anymore. I'm lost for words and spitting feathers. I keep my gob closed and stare out the window at nature. Good old nature. I love nature. It makes everything better.

"You've fucked me about long enough, sunshine!"

Gam-Gam snaps back at me. He has no problem listing the lineage of issues he has with me staying on his farm. I try to interject and stop him from making me feel even worse.

"I don't need to hear…."

"One. Losing the spare key. Two. Drinking and sniffing that shit all of the time. Three. Taking a massive dump on my fucking flower patch. Need I go on, soft boy?"

I can't help but burst out laughing. Then, I start pissing myself, seeing the funny side. A crap on his flower patch is one for the memory bank. How can shit on somebody else's flowers not be considered funny? That little child's voice inside my stupid head begins to chuckle.

"It's not funny."

Even chuffing Gammy Leg has a cheeky little smile on his chubby chops. His upper lip twitching, and gagging to blurt out a tiny giggle. We're both trying to hide our teeth-stained grins like naughty little slags. This manages to ease an agitated situation as the mood in the front room calms.

"I'm really sorry, mate. I'll be on my best behaviour from now on."

"It's too late."

Gammy Leg shakes his head. I can tell in his eyes he's been thinking about this for a while.

"I'm really, really, really sorry."

"Just leave."

Gammy Leg turns his back on me, slowly pointing at the front door.

"Where am I meant to go?"

I ask quietly, secretly scared and very frightened. I've got nowhere else to go. No family. No friends. Nothing. Gammy Leg kicks back and shrugs at me. He's trying to play the big fella, thinking he's Mr Tough Man. That he's solid as a rock.

"I've got nowhere else to go, mate."

"You should have thought about that first."

"You said you would always be there for me?"

"Don't put this one on me, soft boy."

"You said you would have my back no matter what happened."

Gammy Leg calmly defends himself, folding his arms like a spoilt brat. I can't help but shake my head at this family betrayal yet again. Everybody around me is a Judas. I have a hundred stab marks on my back. I'm practically ready to pray at the altar of Gammy Leg, but he won't even look me in the eye.

"You've done this to yourself."

"You promised me you wouldn't abandon me."

"I've given you one, two, three. God knows how many chances?"

"Give me one more chance, please, please let me stay with you."

"I don't know what to say, soft boy."

"Neither do I."

I wait in silence for some kind of answer from him.

"What happened?"

"When?"

"What happened to that nice kid I used to know?"

Gammy Leg looks really disappointed in me. I don't know what to say. I can't honestly answer. So I just shrug and look away.

"That nice kid who used to sit on my knee."

"Yeah, well, he's gone."

I'm not a flipping kid anymore. I try to look away and avoid being made to feel like a child. But unfortunately, I'm always seen as a child, not just by the family but by everyone. Always like I'm a naughty little kid who has committed a crime.

"Sit on my knee and play with my beard, remember that?"

"Yeah."

"I can't think how old you would have been?"

"About five or six."

"You would sit on my knee at your Granny's and be excited to see me."

"Ha! Bloody hell, mate, you've got a good memory."

"Do you not remember, soft boy?"

"Mate, let's not even get into that mess."

"How did we get from sitting on my knee to this?"

"Just let me stay, and I'll put things right. Then, we can move on without mentioning anything from the past. Start fresh and move forward together. Just the two of us, as a new family."

Me and Gammy Leg both stop talking. We look at opposite ends of the room. I've not seen his gentle side in years. Everything is so quiet I can hear ringing in my ears. The wind is howling, and the rank smell from my clothing is forcing its way up my nose.

"Get your stuff together. I've made up my mind, and you need to leave. I don't care where you go. It's got nothing to do with me anymore, soft boy."

"It's got everything to do with you. You're a gross imbecile!"

"What did you just call me?"

Me and Gammy Leg stand at opposite ends of the room, staring at each other like animals getting ready to fight.

"Just because I've taken a shit in your garden, that's why I've got to leave? I've already told you I'd knocked about fifty times, and you wouldn't answer me. So where else was my shit meant to go?"

"I thought you couldn't remember anything?"

Gammy Leg is watching me, trying to catch me out. Have I been caught out? Is my fuzzy memory as cloudy as I've claimed it to be? I need help with words. I've not got a decent comeback. He's tripped me up. Fair play.

"It's not even really about the shit if I'm being honest."

"Ah, finally! The real reason. It's so you can move her onto the farm instead of me?"

"It's not."

Gammy Leg is looking uncomfortable. I'm not the only one with things to hide. Skeletons are shaking around in Gammy Leg's closet too.

"It is, though?"

I'm not letting it drop until I get an honest answer from this gross imbecile.

"It fucking isn't!"

Gammy Leg snaps back and gallops toward me. He towers over my head in the centre of the front room. My nose nearly touching his chest.

"She's not moving in?"

"What?"

"Is she moving in? Yes, or no?"

"It's not relevant."

"Yes, or no?"

"It doesn't matter."

"Of course it matters."

"It doesn't."

"Is she moving in?"

"She is! Yes! Yes, she is! She's fucking moving onto the farm, alright? Happy now?"

Gammy Leg bellows like a fog horn as we both stare down. A pair of wolves and hawks at heart. Looking to pick off the weak sheep from the herd.

"The real reason you're kicking me out is so you can move your little piece in without me around cramping your style."

"Yeah, alright, Pixie is moving in with me. But that's not it. The real reason is you. I can't stand you here any longer, soft boy. You're selfish, reckless, pathetic, and self-pity. It's all you. Even if Pixie wasn't coming, I'd still want you to leave."

The truth is out. Gammy Leg hates me just like everybody else. I feel like the most hated man in the world.

"Right. I'll go upstairs to get my stuff then."

I stand and gaze out of the window, taking in the beauty of nature. The bright blue sky makes me tingle inside. I've been standing there for quite a while. I can hear the animals from a distance. The animals finally talk to one another. An oinky-oinky. A moo-moo-moo. A clucky-clucky.

"What are you thinking about, soft boy?"

"Just thinking about life."

"What about it?"

"I can't wait for it to end."

The room goes very quiet. Everything is silent except trustworthy nature.

"Don't be like that, soft boy. You've got plenty of time left, plenty to live for."

"I'm just here, alone, all of the fucking time. If I don't shout or sniff or drink, I'll cry. I'll cry and cry and cry until I take my last breath."

My eyes fill up with tears.

"I'm long for this world, Gam Gam."

"Don't be so dramatic. Life isn't that bad. You just need to make the most of it."

"I've not enjoyed life since I stopped seeing Lass."

I'm still glaring out the window, looking at the bright blue sky.

"Stop being so bloody daft. Stupid prick."

"Lass hasn't either."

"Now you're really being a silly twat."

"Why?"

"Of course you fucking have."

"I'll do it if I want, mate."

"Do what?"

"End it."

"Ha! Don't be silly."

"I know you want me to."

"Well, I don't, so you're wrong."

"I see the way you look at me."

"When?"

"All of the time.

"I don't."

"You hate me."

"Nah, soft boy."

"You blame me for everything."

I don't know what to say. I'm lost for words. Complete silence. Neither of us says a word. The only sounds are from outside, the howling of the wind and us two fat cunts gasping for breath.

"I saw the way you looked at me."

"When?"

"You want me to leave and to die. You want me to go quick, so you don't have to look after me. It's alright, mate. I want that too."

"I'm not doing this again, soft boy."

I finally turn around for the first time in what feels like hours. Gammy Leg looks down, and he's trying not to cry.

"I'm sorry, mate. I really am."

"Just say it."

"I can't."

"Say it."

"You know I can't."

"All you have to do is say it. It's only three words."

I get on my knees and grab Gammy Legs face with my hands. I push my forehead against his as water streams down my face.

"Just say it. Three words. Repeat after me, and I'll do anything you want. Say, 'I love you,' and I'll help you however you want me to."

I wipe away my tears and stop crying like a little girl. Gammy Leg won't look me in the eye. He points me toward the stairs. I slowly stand up and slump my way up to the cupboard. One step at a time. Gammy Leg buries his round head into his steak-sized hands. I soon drag my packed bag down the stairs. I've got to clear the phlegm from my dry throat to speak. Could murder a bevvy right about now. A little toot of something that will clear my brain box.

"I'll get going then?"

"Fine."

Gammy Leg simply nods in approval.

"I'm sure Granny would be dead proud."

"Meaning?"

"If she knew her perfect saint Gam Gam was kicking me onto the street, would you still be her golden boy?"

"I don't need you giving me life lessons. We both know who the top gaffer is around here, don't we?"

Gammy Leg grins widely. The sun through the window bouncing off of his skull. I've heard enough of his crap. I'm either going to cry or kill him. I contain myself before I do something I truly regret. I'm leaving this dump.

"Hang on a minute."

He calls me back before I storm out and slam the door.

"What?"

I turn to him as I leave, my bag draped over my tense shoulders.

"I don't know what to say, soft boy."

''Neither do I, Gam-Gam.''

I see that Gammy Leg wants to say something but doesn't know how. I sigh, with a pounding headache moving around to my temple and a throat like dry sawdust. I grab hold of my bag straps, ensure I've got my digital pocket pad, nod my head to say goodbye, and walk out the front door. Quietly pulling it shut behind me. The two of us part ways again, two unhappy men left to wallow in self-pity and depression.

HAAAWWWHHH!!!

HAAAWWWHHH!!

HAAAWWWHHH!

CHAPTER 4

The hero never leaves the kingdom without his gold. But I'm not just a hero. I'm Lad, the traveller and dragon slayer of the land. Fuck Odysseus! I'd knock him out no matter how many silly buggers he'd killed in Troy. He would get lippy, so I would smack him straight in the snout. One punch. Then theirs that little bandit Don Quixote. He's a member of the lower mobility, just like me, so I would give him a shove to the cold, hard ground and nick his horse. Don't even get me started on Faust. If that were my soul, I would call it back from the Devil. The Devil would be begging me to take my soul back. I'm this generation's ultimate hero on his epic journey.

I'm sat in the La-di-da, La-di-do, area of runaway carriages, with its comfy seats, tea and biscuits. It doesn't matter as far as the bump and grind of the train goes. Bumping up and down as the train knocks against the tracks. Lass cracks open a tinny of the finest oil as we strap ourselves into this roller-coaster. Lass has a little sip and offers me one. I take the can and have a big gulp of the strong stuff. My face cringes at its strength. Thick oil.

"Ha! You drink oil like a little girl."

Lass points at me and brags about how hard she is for being able to down a drink without nearly being sick. She signals that she's got a bit of cri-cringle-brekk in her pocket. If I'm fleeing, I can really get into it.

Lass nips off to the bog for a quick sniff. Before she left, she had asked me for a key so that she could dip it into her plastic baggy and have a right sniffy-whiff. Her words, not mine. I end up giving her my scissors. She finally reaches the toilet after knocking into everybody she sees. I really hope that she doesn't lose my scissors. I sit and wait for Lass while looking out of the window at the world, gazing at the sights and supping my oil. I glance at the beauty of the fields and farms. A sexy pixie fairy flies past the train. She points at me with her wand and shows me the eye-watering greenery and bright blue skies. These are two of my favourite things in the whole wide world. Images that have never left the depths of my soul. These are the most incredible memories of my life. Surrounded by a gorgeous mix of colours. The pixie fairy lifts up her top and shows me her iddy-biddy-boobies. The pixie fairy gives me the middle finger, laughs, and flies off.

Lass returns to her seat and gives me a big, wet, sloppy kiss on the chops. Can tell that she's been gurning. Everybody on the train ignores us. Lass offers me the cri-cringle-brekk. I down my tin of oil as quickly as possible, trying not to cringe, to impress Lass. I take the sniff from her and get fleeing in the bogs. I take back my scissors and make my way to the shitter. I sway from side to side while starting to feel the effects of the strong can of oil, bumping into every twat in their seats.

"Do you mind?"

This fat, old git turns around and has a go at me.

"Shut it, you fat old git."

He turns away. I win!

I arrive at the toilet, and someone's dropping a log in there by the smell of it. I chomp and bump as I wait and wait. Expecting a big beefy guy to come out, but instead, it's some fit piece. What a flipping beauty. One criticism I have of the lady is that she's left a right-smelly one in the bog. She's a stunning redhead, dyed red, not natural, who's left skids down the bowl. I go into the toilet and prep myself to get fleeing. I put my scissor tips into the plastic bag of cri-cringle-brekk, get a good fatty of white powder on the tip, pull it out and up to my left nostril, and sniff as hard as possible. I get a massive dose of phlegm stuck in my throat. I sniff up again as hard as possible and spit into the sink. I check myself in the bog mirrors, put the bag and scissors back into my pocket, and leave. I begin to feel really, really fleeing as I walk back to my seat, everybody looking at me, completely aware of what me and Lass are doing. Shaking their heads in disgust.

"You should be ashamed of yourself!"

This skinny young tart looks up and shakes her head at me.

"Pipe down, you skinny young tart."

I get back to my seat. Lass is sat with her trotters up on my chair. I cough to get her to move. Which she reluctantly does. We both sit opposite each other. Lass does her own thing. I do mine.

"Ding! Ding! Ding!"

The digital and interconnected loudspeakers throughout the train begin to play. An announcement is to be made.

"This is your driver speaking, Mercury/Sagittarius. We'll be pulling into the final destination in about ten minutes."

Me and Lass glare at the speakers and roll our eyes. Lass disappears back to the bog for yet another toot. She doesn't ask for my scissors, so…I'm guessing she'll use her finger and have a gummy? I'm slapping and chapping my lips together and gurning my nut off. Chewing my tongue and sniffing. As the train bumps, grinds, and gets ready to pull into the city station, Lass is still gone. We screech into the city as scrounges scowl and chuck their shoes at the train. I nip to the bog to check where she is. I lightly knock on the door while the other passengers are getting off.

"Lass? Lass? Lass?"

My sweetheart isn't answering me. I thud and bang on the door.

"Lass! We're here!"

Still no answer. I'll have to kick the bastard door down if it. I see the four-eyed Mercury/Sagittarius moron conducting the herd onto the platform. Me and lovely Lass can't be getting locked on and ending up back on the land. I check the door, and it's open. I barge in, and nobody's there. Where the hell is Lass? I start to get a mini sweat on, I'm worried, but I have no other choice. I stumble off the train onto the shitty city platform. I jog alongside to see if I can see her. But nothing. Lass has gone, and I don't know where?

I check my jacket pocket. Thankfully, I've still got hold of my scissors. I make my way out of the city station, and still no sign of Lass. So where the hell is my gorgeous girlfriend? I hope that she's wondering where I am too?

At least she left the tins behind. I hold four in my hand and crack one open. Argh. Thick, gooey oil. I walk through the colossal city station. A virtual universe. Giant screens as big as trucks, echoing noises as loud as street parades, yellow flashing lights as bright as fireworks. Everything is now completely digital and technological, requiring very little from anyone. More importantly, everybody is tracked, traced, and monitored everywhere. I quickly drink a wee tinny. It's boiling. I make my way out of the station and see Lass standing right in front of me! Lass pulls the baggy out of her pocket. She doesn't give a rat's ass. I hand over my rusty scissors, surprised and buzzing. She dips the tip into the baggy, brings the white powder to her nose, and sniffs up. She passes me the equipment. We both stagger around the front of the station like a couple of chickens that have just been fucked. We laugh and kiss, laugh and kiss, laugh and kiss. Then Lass drops to the ground, her head bouncing off the concrete. She starts spazzing out. Shaking and foaming at the mouth, making terrifying moans. I look around. Everybody is gathered in a circle, filming us on their pads, pointing, uploading us.

HAAAWWWHHH!!!
HAAAWWWHHH!!
HAAAWWWHHH!

"What happens after that?"

"What?"

"What happens after the seizure?"

"I wake up."

"Always in the same place?"

"I always come out of it in the exact same place."

"Do I die?"

"I've not got a clue. I snap straight up."

"What do you think it means?"

"What do any of the trips mean."

"And this is every time?"

"Nah, no, not every time, but at least a couple of trips per week."

"Are we always on a train?"

"Yes."

"I don't have anything like that. I'm knocked out when my head hits that floor until I shoot out."

"You never trip?"

"Once or twice."

"Lucky you."

"You have some crazy one's babe."

"Yep."

"I wasn't going to bring this up until we'd run out of the white powder. But I tell you what, I've got some new shit. I was going to surprise you when we finished the white. I can go chop us out a couple lines. Sort your noggin out?"

"What is it, and who did you get it from?"

"I got it half price from Teleport Boy."

"I'm not sure."

"Come on, babe, it's way better than the white."

“Err, fine, go on then. I just hope I don’t float off to the land of the fucking trains and stations and spazzing out.”

“I’ll be back in a bit.’’

Lass has finally left the room. Jogging out the door like a flock of irritated pigeons towards mouldy bread. She’s endlessly droning on and on so that our broken skulls cannot manage to cope any longer. She thinks that I want cri-cringle-brekk all of the time. She likes it twenty-four-seven, even at this time in the morning. Maybe it calms her shaky nerves and suppresses her trembling fears. Perhaps it clears her confusion and darkness. It doesn’t do that for me. It turns my psyche darker and darker to the point of no return. I’ve committed many crimes and sins within that surrealist nightmare world. When morality has broken down in real life, no stone is left unturned when your eyes are closed. There are more crazy neurons firing around my psyche than atoms in space. I don’t think I’ve slept past the sun rising in years. Sometimes Lass does. But not me. Sometimes Lass carelessly wakes me up an hour earlier than the sun when she’s hot and bothered after a steamy dream. She jams my hand into her creamy wetness before she nods back off and leaves me with a stomach of sticky spunk to wash off my flab. I cup it in my right hand and rub it on the floor until it disappears like a ghost at night. Lass is even more of an addict than me. She's more into her drugs. I'm a day drinker.

Lass had attempted suicide three times, not in the flat, but before we moved here. I just think that it's a ridiculous term to use. There's no such thing as attempting to commit suicide. Especially three times. We know how to kill ourselves. If we want to do it, we will hang ourselves. Jump off a very high building. Cut our throats. We know how to kill ourselves effectively, instantly, and quickly. So, to claim that we've attempted to kill ourselves doesn't sit with me. Never mind three times.

I lean against the armchair in my white kegs. Used to the cold. Neither the blankets nor my kegs are pristine and clean. Both with soaking damp marks and rank brown stains. I use the chair to straighten my back and a pillow to rest my tin tray. Lass barges back in through the door, wearing her white kegs, while our remaining underwear and clothing need to be washed. Lass has tape wrapped around her chest to make a weird bra. She leans beside me and spreads some glowing purple powder from her creased-up, see-through baggy all over the tray. Using a sharp blade to chop up the purple into dust. She cuts me a thick, fat line and brings the tray to my nose as I sniff the dust through a roll of brown card. My eyes pop wide open as my nose swells and puffs sideways. My teeth begin to grate, back and forth, back and forth, back and forth. My lips start to swish and tingle. Swish! Swish! Swish! Argh, my eyes! Argh, my eye! My piss pots are watering. I try to stumble up, push the tray away, and wipe the tears in my window reflection.

"What is it, babe? Why are you being such a little puss-puss?"

"My…eyes…wet."

I manage to rub the tears from my blinkers. I sniff up even more and start to truly mong out. I stumble and fall around the cramped space where we're forced to sleep. The feeling in my legs begins to evaporate. I look around, and the whole place has turned bright red and dark green. The colours shine and flicker as my hands transform into a child's drawings. I'm a chubby stick drawing. I drop onto my back and stare at the ceiling. All of my limbs lose their feeling and sensation. Even the tingles evaporate as I spaz out, as my consciousness becomes one with the world of my colourful cartoon flat. Lass rambles on and on. But all I can hear is the sound of babble, babble, babble.

"I'll chop one out for myself."

I mong out on the floor and just about manage to turn my head to the right side. Lass is in her undercrackers, chopping out an even fatter line, thicker than anything I'd ever seen. Way puffier than the one which I had taken. I want to tell her to be careful. But I can't. She usually gets the white stuff. The purple cri-cringle-brekk is so much stronger. I don't think that she will be able to handle it. Lass sniffs the holy shit out of the dust through the rotting rolled-up card.

"Argh! Argh!"

Lass follows my lead as she goes to the shattered window reflection to wipe her piss holes. I look around the flat. Everything is still part of this red and green glowing universe.

Lass rips the tape from her nipples, pulls down her pants, and starts masturbating violently before she collapses on her back next to me. We both look up at the ceiling. Love and beauty. Peace and love.

After what feels like a lifetime, we're both awake and talking again. I put on some dirty joggers and a crappy T-shirt. As does Lass. We both sit on the floor as the sickening purple cri-cringle-brekk dust rests on the tray.

"That was incredible."

Lass stretches back against the door and rolls around on the floor.

"Yep."

She was right. That stuff was pure class. I don't know where we both went. Beyond this constricted reality. It was a unique and gorgeous land of vibrating colour. Lass lifts herself up and relaxes her head onto my shoulder.

"How was it so strong?"

"I sacrificed a lot to get hold of the purple."

Neither of us ask how she got it. Or what she had to do to get it. I'm sure that Teleport Boy wasn't too harsh on her.

"The purple is the next level."

"Wait until I get some of the red dust."

"Red! Fucking hell. Strong?"

"The strongest ever made. Let's just say that the purple is nothing in comparison. It will send us into a completely different dimension, and we may not return."

I peel Lass's head from my shoulder and wobble on my feet. I trip down onto my knees and have to crawl up the sides of the wall. I claw and gasp my way to the side of our flat. I pick up a tinned flask of water and have a big swig to get rid of my dry mouth. I half answer any questions with a mouth full of water. Gaggling as spit drips from my gob and onto the floor. I slowly lower my tinned flask onto the side as we hear an unbearably loud thud at the door. It only seems fitting that Lass is the one to drop everything and answer the door. She gives me sharp daggers and gallops out of the room. I keep it casual. None of the clothes we're wearing are ours. I've not brought anything for quite a long time. Nobody wears clothes like this anymore. I just happened to find them in town where the old cinema used to be. I crouched down to see the rubble and saw a silver strap bag with old-time civil war gear. It looked and smelt pretty clean, depending on your standards. You find some great stuff if you mooch around what used to be the old city streets and stumble by any of the senior civil war time places. Shops, bars, cinemas, and restaurants are all gone, but plenty of stuff left for us, new ones. Clothes, flasks, tins of food, and bottles of alcohol.

I can hear Lass laughing. Who the hell is it? Who the fuck is outside? It could be one of those spotty, rank, fat whores? On the other hand, Vanilla Sykes could be trying to hand over another sex baby. After completing the grotty assault course around the flat, I drop down the stairs and barge through the front door. Yet again, I stumble over my feet and see this weedy-looking nerd talking to Lass. He's balding on top with curls at the back and sides, a huge forehead, big nose, manky teeth, gigantic black glasses, wearing a really old-time brown suit, white socks pulled all the way up, and black shoes. Lass introduces us to one another.

"This is X-Y. He works for Monsieur – long live the great Monsieur!"

X-Y cleans the saliva from the corners of his dried-out mouth with his long fingernails. I at least bite my nails off. The grubby little git. He tips his thick glasses back into the centre after they have slanted to the point of hanging from his face.

"Anyway, what can I do for you, mate?"

X-Y starts to search through his brown suit pockets, starting from the top and working his way down. It's like a clown performance. He'll begin juggling his own testicles next.

"Oh no!"

"What is it X-Y?"

Lass interrupts as though she knows him. Maybe that's where she got the purple. Whoring herself out to the men of Monsieur – long live the great Monsieur! - I give her wide eyes to tell her to shut her big bastard gob.

"Calm down. I've found it."

X-Y holds up sheets of stained, crumpled paper. Only a person with glasses as big and hideous as those could read torn-up works.

"The papers were in my shoes. They don't fit me properly."

I invite Mr Floppy Shoes into the flat. Lass slumps to the floor. Mr Floppy Shoes starts speaking nonsense. He seems sure I know why he's here, but I haven't got a flipping scooby-doo.

"Are you going to tell us why you're here, mate?"

I slowly start to get on the defensive and quietly move away from him. Mr Floppy Shoes is just an act. I scan the flat. There are a few blades still about the place. Lass just sits there. I stare at Mr Floppy Shoes. I wait for him to speak. He grins like a little weasel. A pussy cat with a broom handle shoved up its rut. I give a light smile to show some manners. Mr Floppy Shoes straightens his glasses and takes a deep breath.

"I'm just here to do a routine check for Monsieur – long live the great Monsieur!"

"What check-up?"

"Monsieur – long live the great Monsieur! - needs these forms signing to say that you were here when I came to see you. It's only a routine check-up for those in the area."

Mr Floppy Shoes stands beside me with grubby, soaking-wet papers dangling over my head. He lets out one of his ridiculous smiles again.

"That's it!"

I dive across the flat, pinning Mr Floppy Shoes against the wall.

"Babe!"

"Please, don't hurt me sir, please, don't hurt me."

"It's fine, X-Y, everything is fine."

Lass sits back down and watches me with awe. She trusts that I know what I'm doing. I grab him by the throat with my right hand and leave my left to dingle-dangle-doo by my side.

Using all of my weight to keep Mr Floppy Shoes held in place. I make him stare into the abyss. Glare into the darkness which fills my soul. I enjoy the fear in his eyes as he sees the firing flames in mine.

"Just answer me one question, Mr Floppy Shoes. Please, there's no need to be scared. Do us both the good grace to answer one question? One question, one ickle-wickle question, and we'll let you leave. We'll sign your papers and never see each other again."

"Yes, anything, please, don't hurt me, I'm just doing my job."

I loosen my grip and let the poor man breathe. He takes a lot of deep breaths, and we both wait until he's calmed down. We're so pleasant and courteous when it comes to the welfare of others. Especially lovely Lass. She's such a generous and selfless sweetheart.

"Ask him the question, babe. Ask him! Ask him! Ask him!"

"Are you ready for the one and only question, Mr Floppy Shoes? Then, it's time…drum roll please…for your one and only question!"

He nods in all of the right places. I step back, careful not to tread on glass or broken box pieces. Mr Floppy Shoes catches his breath and straightens his tie.

"Mr Floppy Shoes?"

He clears his throat, looks down at the ground, takes a lot of deep breaths, and tries to avoid eye contact. Mentally preparing himself. We both keep a straight face. Lass begins to hideously laugh and hysterically clap her hands. She absolutely loves it.

"Please, just ask me."

"Count me down, my lovely Lass."

"Three! Two! One!"

I slowly inch in closer to Mr Floppy Shoes. I whisper directly into his ugly face.

"Is your name really X-Y? Do you actually work for Monsieur – long live the great Monsieur! Or are you trying to scam us?"

He looks at me, confused.

"It is my name. X-Y is my name. I honestly do work for Monsieur – long live the great Monsieur!"

"Can I see some proof, please, my good chap?"

"What about his community ID, babe?"

"Odoo! You are the smart one, lovely Lass, aren't you?"

"Anything for you."

Terrified. Shaking. Trembling. Coughing. Crying.

He empties every pocket as fast as he possibly can. Clumsy fool, we smirk at his god-awful dress sense. I look down at the floor. All I can see are the crumbled documents. Then, finally, he produces his ID.

"Mr Floppy Shoes, would you be so kind as to tell us what that is on the floor?"

"It's my community ID card. I promise, I promise."

Me and Lass gaze at each other before staring at Mr Floppy Shoes. I nod my head to direct him to pick up his own ID.

"Does this ID confirm what you've told us?"

"It does, it does."

Mr Floppy Shoes begins to shake and cry. He lifts up his community ID, slowly and delicately turns it around, and shows it to us. I quickly snatch the card out of Mr Floppy Shoe's hands and stand up straight with my shoulders back.

"Well, well, well. Who would have thought it."

"What does it say, babe? What does it say?"

"His name is X-Y, and he works for Monsieur – long live the great Monsieur!"

"He was telling us the truth?"

"Yep."

"Good."

"Pencil!"

Lass quickly passes me a pencil. I hand the card back to Mr Floppy Shoes, who quickly and tightly puts on every item of clothing. I lean down towards the grubby papers and sign them. I hand them back to Mr Floppy Shoes. He puts everything back into his old crumpled brown suit and hurries toward the door. He looks terrified on his way out.

I lunge with both hands to grab the back of his collar. I drag him, kicking and yelping, away from the door and onto the floor. I have a firm grip on the scruff of his neck. He's scared and crying. I get down on the floor next to Lass. We stare at each other with big grins on our faces. I hold him down, gripping the back of his jacket to the floor so he can't escape. Lass quickly grabs the plastic baggy of purple cri-cringle-brekk, and she jumps on top of him. She wraps her legs around him in a riding position while I grip both his wrists and pin his arms over his head to stop him from getting away or moving. Lass pushes all her weight onto Mr Floppy Shoes, enough so that she can get his legs to stop kicking. Lass scratches his eyes with her long fingernails, which makes him scream! His gob is open, she tips the entire bag of purple cri-cringle-brekk into his mush. Mr Floppy Shoes begins to choke and gasp for air. As I hold him down, Lass pinches his big nose with her two fingers, closing his mouth with her other hand. After a few moments of pushing and wriggling, Mr Floppy Shoes stops moving.

Then he stops breathing.

Mr Floppy Shoes is dead. Another body for our ever-growing pile of corpses. We'll have to find another hiding place to put him.

Me and Lass both stare at the glass bottle on the floor.

Lass smashes the glass. She throws me a thick piece and picks up one for herself. We both stand over Mr Floppy Shoes and begin to undress him.

"Let me do it."

"What about the blood?"

"I'm starting to really like the blood, babe."
HAAAWWWHHH!!!
HAAAWWWHHH!!
HAAAWWWHHH!

CHAPTER 5

I try my hardest to avoid any bright flickers. Thank God almighty Jesus that the light isn't too strong. I can keep my piss holes open, at least for now. There's a kicky-wicky camera implanted in the top of this huge white scanner, which is about two inches above my snout. Panicking will only make things worse. My arms are tucked into my sides, and my legs are stretched straight out. I'm lying on my back and looking at this mechanical structure I've been forced to stay in. These twat-heads, have been testing me with scans, injecting me with druggish liquid, and poking at me with tools. They've been treating me like a captured wild animal. Beaten and butchered in my cage. My captures tell me that they're testing me for my own good. To help me, that's what they've been telling me. That's why I'm induced, recorded, tested, and monitored.

The top of my head is in agony. My long scar shoots and shocks from the centre of my head to just above the top of my neck. I try my best not to panic but have to admit to myself quietly that I feel scared. I want to shout at these horrible bastards to let me out of this machine, but I don't want to set off the alarms again. I know how to behave myself. I can't handle them poking and prodding me. What the hell is happening to me? Is my life coming to an end? Maybe dying is better than whatever this is. I imagine that death is a gift compared to this bollocks.

After what feels like forever, they finally use a device to speak to me. A small microphone has been inserted into the structure, buzzing from just above the scar on the top of my head. A sexy voice begins speaking to me. She sounds very young and incredibly chirpy.

"Are you OK in there?"

"Yes."

I clear my throat and respond to the microphone above.

"You're doing really well. We just need you in there for a bit longer, and then you're free to come out. Is that OK?"

"Yes."

"We just need you to answer a couple of questions."

"OK."

"We want you to close your eyes as soon as you see a red-light flash from above. Do you understand?"

"Yes."

"You're doing really well."

A red light quickly starts flashing above my eyes. I have no choice but to squeeze my blinkers shut, as it's so bright the brightness feels like it could burn through my eyeballs.

"They're closed!"

I shout into the microphone to confirm that I've followed the instructions. The voice changes. It's now a bloke speaking to me. What happened to Doctor Sexy Voice? This new guy sounds like a geezer or a member of a gang.

"Take a few deep breaths and tell us what you can see."

"OK."

I don't appreciate Doctor Geezer telling me what to do. Did he push Doctor Sexy Voice out of the way? Regardless, I take three deep breaths. One. Out. Two. Out. Three. Out. Images start to pop into my head very clearly.

"I can see a hand."

"What kind of hand? Male? Female?"

"Yeah! Man, it's a big and fat man-hand."

The images keep popping into my head. Faster, faster, faster, faster.

"What can you see now? Anything different or still the hand?"

"A lady's neck. She's wearing a gold necklace."

"You're doing really well."

Doctor Sexy Voice takes over to tell me that I'm doing well. I knew that she wouldn't fuck off and leave me with Doctor Geezer. He must have held her away from the microphone. She's too kind and soft for that kind of behaviour. Doctor Sexy Voice would never abandon anybody, especially patients in need. I don't understand why she doesn't run the centre.

"I see a knife. It's a huge knife."

"Keep going."

Doctor Geezer returns, and he tells me to keep going, the cunt! He's keeping my Doctor Sexy Voice away from me.

"A front room, with a whirlpool of blood, the words 'family circle' are written all over the walls, in this thick blood. Wow! A photo of me is hung on the wall and smeared in blood. It looks like me as a kid in a photo frame. Wow! A photo of a young girl, also a kid, she's cute, she's hung up on the wall next to me, the blood oozes over our frames, and we disappear. Wow! Another photo of this girl and me, we're together, and the photo frames quickly disappear into the walls of blood. Rows and rows of different eyes and noses are attached together, a weird-looking short couple, an old couple with lots of wrinkles, a fat man holding the hand of a really skinny girl in just her pants, huge eyes reading a huge book. The skinny girl stretches across my vision with her tits out, disappearing into the whirlpool of blood. Multiple signs, each pointing different ways, toward the wall of blood, a sign which reads family and one which says death."

"You're doing fantastic."

"Black and white cell bars wrapped around both of the signs, all of the eyes and noses split up, they follow the different signs. Death and family, death and family, death and family. Both signs lead everything into the thick whirlpool of blood."

I'm gasping for air, I'm gasping for air, I'm gasping for air.

Another knife, sharp, stab! Gravestones, stab! Stab! Knife, sharp, stab! Grave stones, stab! Stab! Knife, sharp, stab! Grave stones, stab! Stab! Knife, sharp, stab! Grave stones, stab! Stab! Knife, sharp, stab! Grave stones, stab! Stab! Knife, sharp, stab! Grave stones, stab! Stab! Knife, sharp, stab! Grave stones, stab! Stab!"

The bright red light slowly stops flashing. Slowly, slowly, slowly.

I'm struggling to catch my breath. I'm dripping with sweat, I open my piss-holes, and they slowly pull me out of the structure using an electronic handle. Where's my Doctor Sexy Voice?

The Doctors huddle into a circle. Fuck you! What about me? One of the Red-headed female nurses walks me from the bed to a big chair. One slow step at a time. I sit in this black chair with my back straight. I cough and exhale loudly to get my speech back. The redhead gets me a cup of water. I gulp the water down and return to my coughing and exhalation.

"They'll be with you in a minute. Would you like some more water?"

"Yes, please."

I nod and watch from my chair. It feels like a throne. I feel important, like a prince. All of the doctors are acting very seriously. Everything seems dramatic. I'm sitting up straight and feeling calm. Peaceful as I watch over my disciples in their white lab coats. I can stretch out my royal back and noble limbs as much as I want to. I feel very in control like I'm the one who gets to choose when we speak. It's me answering all of their questions. Redhead returns with my water, which I down in one go. The redhead smiles at me. The doctors, about six of them, walk over to my throne.

"How are you feeling? Are you OK?"

It's Doctor Sexy Voice! She's actually a black-haired Asian with glasses.

"Yeah, I'm alright, thanks."

"Glad to hear it. You did really well."

"Thanks."

She smells so lovely, like fresh lavender. I bet she tastes nice too. She ticks all of the boxes of the holy trilogy, sexy voice, fantastic smell, delicious taste.

"Are you ready for a quick test?"

The top of my head starts to hurt, fuck, it's my scar again, fuck, excruciating, fuck, I hold my forehead in my hands, fuck.

"What do you need?"

Doctor Sexy Asian checks on me, putting her tiny, delicate fingers on my back. She has a big heart, is selfless, and puts others before herself. She may be the one for me. I think it's fate that we're meant to be together.

"Maybe he needs a few hours to recover?"

She's trying to look after me, yet again, I've never been cared for like this while at the centre. She should run this place.

"No, we need to test him now. Dig straight into those perceptions and memories."

This bald prick pipes up, Doctor Bald Bastard, shutting down my Doctor Sexy Asian. I'll kill him. How dare he try to split apart our relationship? Can he not see that I'm in pain and that only Doctor Sexy Asian can help me get better.

"Are you OK with coming with us for some more testing?"

I nod in agreement, only because she politely and friendly asked me. The pain on the top of my head has gone, and I feel fine now. Doctor Sexy Asian's magic touch.

"If you'd like to come with us."

"Yep."

"Take your time to get out of your chair."

I push myself up swiftly from my throne.

Next thing I know, I'm in some cramped room. At least half the size of the lab, claustrophobic box spaces. A completely new set of different specialists are now with me. All other doctors, including Doctor Sexy Asian, my future wife, have chosen to stay in the lab. I imagine she is waiting for me to finish with these twats, getting herself sexually aroused. She's probably wet just thinking about me.

"Do you remember why you're here?"

"Well, err, no, I don't remember."

I just agree with whatever bullshit gibberish they're blabbing. But in all honesty, nobody is making much sense. Even me. We're all putting on this vast performance. I've got the lead role. I rub the back of my head while I attempt to take in what they're trying to say.

"Blah, blah, blah, blah, blah, blah, blah, blah, blah, blah, blah."

They've all stopped speaking English. Maybe I can't speak English anymore, perhaps I'm in the Far East with Doctor Sexy Asian, and they're teaching my wife's native tongue.

"Blah, blah, blah, blah, blah, blah, blah, blah, blah, blah, blah."

I scan the room, tracing the cameras from the corner of my peepholes. They love to watch my every move. I see what looks like a small orange sticker stuck to the door. I look to my left and see the same orange writing stuck on the top corner of the wall. Without asking these toffs, I get up, go to the orange writing on the door, and read it aloud. I gaze at it with wonder. It looks very familiar and brings on a feeling of awe, sickness, and disgust.

'Monsieur Corporations.'

HAAAWWWHHH!!!

HAAAWWWHHH!!

HAAAWWWHHH!

CHAPTER 6

Granny, now in her early seventies, comes stomping through the front door, carrying a bucket full of water. She holds the bucket by the handle in her right hand while gripping a yellow sponge in the left. Granny is wearing a flowery dress like she's going somewhere important. I stomp, dragging my swollen feet like a toddler, into the centre of the front room, thudding behind Granny. I've piled on a shit ton of weight since getting kicked off Gammy Legs farm. The radicalisation of my own body has been fluctuating, up and down, for the past year. This has caused the excessive stretching of my skin, back and forth, back and forth, back and forth, until thick, deep, dark, purple marks and long lines have scarred my body, like a swollen burn victim or melted candle wax figure. Fuck me sideways, I'm out of breath, but I need to calm her down. I wear my classic black shorts, a black T-shirt, a hoodie, and socks as usual.

Granny has this massive façade. She wants to come across as this big and strong family leader. She strides like a snake oil salesman, a hairy street con man, even in her old age. I offer the grumpy old goat a moment to calm herself. She grunts and tuts like a broken musical instrument. Granny is raging. She's somehow still holding the bucket in one hand, the sponge in the other, getting drips of water onto the stained carpet.

"Granny, just relax."

"Relax?"

"They're only words."

I'm too exhausted for her crap. This has happened a million times before. She whines like a thirteen-year-old virgin starting her first period.

"Only bastard words?'"

I collapse back onto the sofa. Standing or walking is boring. What's the point.

"They're not only words."

"Some daft kids will have done it."

Granny pretends to find it hilarious, cackling like a green-faced witch flying over the rooftops on her broomstick. I just stare at her blankly. I'm used to seeing this eccentric behaviour. She looks out the window, side to side, looking out for the scoundrels. I shrug it off.

"Granny, listen, there's no need to get yourself so worked up."

"They can't even spell properly."

"It's only a bit of writing. Just forget about them."

"I'm sick of this."

Granny turns away from me and tries to keep herself together. Playing the victim, the narcissistic fool, always the victim. I reluctantly peel my bloated body from the sofa. I try to console Granny. I attempt to put my hand on her shoulder, but she lightly brushes it off and shuffles to the other end of the room. Still clinging onto her trustworthy bucket and sponge.

"I'll try to scrub the rest."

I flop back onto the sofa, wriggling about to get comfy. This sofa is flipping ancient. Granny's had it for as long as I can remember. I swear some dust blew off the arms. I stare at the walls. The wallpaper is still peeling off, with its grubby edges and soaking wet texture. I'm constantly telling Granny to stop being such a lazy bitch and get the wall sorted out. She says we have to wait for it to dry out. ''We can't fix a wall which hasn't dried out.'' If it hasn't dried out in all these years, it isn't going to do it by itself. You can tell that somebody used to smoke in this gaff. The ceiling is brown, and the room still stinks of fags

"Come on, get dressed. There's a good boy."

I'm not a boy, bitch. I'm a grown man. Granny goes to leave.

"Give your room a quick tidy when you go upstairs. A little spray, it stinks in there."

"Of what?"

"Sweat and shit."

"Fine."

I know that my hygiene routine could have been better.

"Don't forget to take your meds. We don't want a repeat of last time."

"I won't forget to take them. Just stop nagging me."

She's finally pissed off and left me to it. I take my digital pocket pad out of my black hoodie and make no effort to get dressed, still wearing my shorts and T-shirt. I soon become occupied with this silly pad. We're now at the stage, even within the land, in which to participate in your own community, you have to be hooked up, to some extent, to the digital tracking grid. Set up by tech-mogul, Monsieur – long live the great Monsieur!

Prancing Pixie comes fluttering into the front room like a beautiful fairy. She's dressed in a pink costume with cute wings and a silver tiara. A tiny and terrifyingly skinny blonde, roughly four-foot-nine in height, banging bright blue eyes that sparkle alongside her glistening white teeth.

"Hi, Pixie."

"Hello."

"Nice outfit."

"Thanks!"

"You're welcome."

"Do I look sexy?"

"Err, I'm, err, I'm not sure…."

"Do you think Gam Gam will enjoy it?"

"Probably."

"A sexy Pixie fairy makes him very hard."

"Interesting."

"I wore this, especially for Gam Gam."

"Gross imbecile."

"What?"

"Nothing, Pixie. Have you been behaving yourself?"

"Of course."

Her frail and pale figure makes her look like a teenage smackhead. Like Tinkerbell, if she was to smoke crack. This troubled girl is Gammy Leg's thirteen-year-old girlfriend. Teeny-weeny Pixie suffers from anorexic tendencies. Anorexia is all the range, especially in teenagers. It's constantly promoted online. You can't go online without seeing what people call a 'kiddie starving challenge.' The girls can get away with almost anything if they make a preachy point. Pixie got so much abuse, from her fellow teens, for only starving herself. She was bullied online until she became bulimic. To stop all of the online hate and make herself famous again.

Pixie lives with forty-seven-year-old Gammy Leg on his farm. They met on a dating website quite a while back, meeting up after chatting briefly and shagging in Gammy Leg's barn. He really gave her one! He showed me a video of her riding him. Now, I wouldn't exactly consider Pixie to be a tarted whore, but she was on her back, legs in the air, and on Gammy Leg's barn floor within a matter of weeks. Gammy Leg thinks that he's hit the jackpot. Pixie only likes sex with Gammy Leg if it can be filmed and posted for all to see. Her attention-obsessed mate's rate and critiques how well the teen can keep up with a gross imbecile such as Gammy Leg.

I remember him telling me.

"Here, soft boy."

"What?"

"Look at me, shagging this girl."

"How old she is?"

"Never you mind, soft boy."

I've always been creeped out by how much younger Pixie is. But a sexual moralistic framework doesn't exist since life went online. That's old-time fuddy-duddy dinosaur crap.

Pixie has been staying with Granny for a few days while following her medical requirements regarding food. Otherwise, she could end up back in the isolated hell hole for months. Granny has taken on the role of parent to Pixie. The two of them naturally and unquestioningly adopt the roles of mother and daughter. I'm surprised I've not walked in on Granny breastfeeding Pixie from her saggy old boobs. Clearly, Gammy Leg isn't giving her enough to suck on. This breastfeeding scenario really could become a reality. I wouldn't be the one to film it, but I'd watch it to gain points on my monthly credit score.

Prancing Pixie hops like a little rabbit around the room, wearing her revealing pink short pyjamas. She is excited, writing and reading notes aloud on her pad. Then, Pixie quickly and eloquently twirls away from me like a ballerina. Half of her bum cheek slides out of her incredibly short PJs. I pretended I didn't see her ass flap out and her cheeks bobbing. There's only one ass that I'm interested in, and that's Lass. I really wish that she was here with me. That she was allowed back. To Granny's, at the very least. I always thought it would be me that wouldn't be allowed back into this family unit.

Granny comes tripping and trampling back into the front room. I can see that this is where Gammy Leg gets his herd stamping from like a pair of hungry hippos.

"I only managed to wash half of it off, the daft buggers. So you're both still not dressed?"

Granny tries to lighten the mood by teasing me.

"You look exactly like your dad! Sat on your flabby ass, messing about like a lazy Larry."

I try my best not to let the silly cow bother me.

"Especially around your chubby little mush-mush, very round and moon shaped. You should watch some of Pixie's old anorexia videos. You could go viral as the fatty-bum-bum-boy who lost it all. Here, you could teach Pixie to put on some weight, and she could teach you to lose it?"

Granny tries to get a reaction from us both. I could punch her straight in the mouth. But I don't. I just think about it.

"I think he gets it. He knows that he's got fat chops. We all know that."

Pixie pipes up and comes to my defence...well...sort of...but not really. More of a dig at Granny than helping me out.

"I wasn't talking to you, little Pixie-pie!"

Granny bites back at Pixie, a ravaging dog foaming at the mouth with rabies.

"You keep telling him that he looks like his dad? He isn't going to know what his dad looks like, is he?"

Granny looks straight through Pixie, and she completely ignores her. Granny starts to walk away, mumbling to herself.

"Your dad hated you from the day that you were born."

This comes from the woman who has never said 'I love you' to anybody within the family. She hates Lass the most. She oozes resentment and contempt for beautiful Lass. Which is whacky and bizarre, as Lass is easily the kindest of the family unit. I'm pretty sure it has something to do with me and Lass not having the same dad.

"My chest is panting, beating so fast. Reach for some water, this isn't a laugh."

Pixie comes out with a line from her stupid poem.

Granny bursts out laughing! A very loud, performative, hideous witch's cackle. Her gob is wide open, so everybody can see what she had for breakfast, her false teeth slapping together.

Chip Fat Mam, and my dad, stayed together for quite a while. Even getting married, until he ran off and started fucking some other woman. Gone forever. Granny took on the role of parent. Gammy Leg played the brother. While Chip Fat Mam went from boyfriend to boyfriend, deadwood relationship to deadwood relationship, eventually meeting Lass's Dad, who left from the very start before Lass was born. Lass stayed living with Chip Fat Mam and her many boyfriends.

"Eaten much this morning, Pixie-poo-poo?"

What would the pair of them be like in a fight? Granny's weight would give her the upper hand, but Pixie would have more stamina and be able to whip out more moves. A girly wrestling match right at my feet. Slip them both into some sexy undercrackers and watch them scrap.

"Why don't you have a fight?"

They both stare at me as though I mean it. I shrug and laugh.

"Shut up, you daft twat! I'm asking skinny-minnie what she's eaten today."

"Ugh! What?"

Pixie groans and moans in response. It actually sounds quite sexy.

"Have you put anything into your tiny mush?"

Granny makes little rabbit noises and carrot signs with her arthritic claws.

"I'm, you know, just not hungry."

Pixie nervously replies. This subject is very touchy, pulling at her PJs and twirling hair around her fingers.

"Pixie-poo-poo ate eight raw carrots last night. Eating raw carrot, after raw carrot. I thought that you'd turned into a rabbit."

Granny thinks she's a stand-up comedian. She's more like a transsexual stripper. If she's to be compared to a performative act, it's definitely a trans pole dancer.

"Just one after the other, after the other, after the other. Greedy gutty-wutts. You'll be as fat as this pig soon."

"I didn't feel like eating."

"Have you slept? You look shattered."

"Yes."

"Or was our Gam Gam up all night making one of those slutty videos you show to all your mates? It's not good for our Gam Gam. I don't know why you force him to do it, Pixie."

Granny is a first-class wind-up merchant. Pixie has learned not to show her tears and fears in public anymore. Yawning and stretching, far and wide. Her PJs are so short I can nearly see a flap flopping out of the front.

This family breakdown led to Lass and me falling in love. Our first hug. Our first date. Our first kiss. Our first fuck. I guess that's why Granny and Chip Fat Mam have banned us from seeing each other. Lass can't come here, and I can't go there. We've tried to make it work behind everybody's back. It was me who taught Lass how to handle her first period. We both experimented and experienced the flow and rivers of blood together. Drip, drip, like a leaking tap out of Lass's fanny. The pair of us lovingly inspected it like a decapitated dead body.

I finally peel my fatty figure off the sofa.

"Take your meds before you go upstairs."

Granny orders me towards my stash. A spoonful of medicine. Tick. A quick squirt up the nostrils. Tick. Swallow my pills without water. Tick

"Done."

As I leave and close the room door, I hear Granny slag me off to Pixie. I look through a little crack in the door.

"He just lounges around the gaff. He needs to finally get off of those awful meds. I don't know why they gave him such a high dose."

Pixie struggles for words, playing with her pigtails out of awkwardness. She has no idea what to say. The same uncomfortable silence fills the room. Silence is always present whenever Granny and Pixie aren't parading around the room and showing off like prostitutes on a street corner. I can't stand to look at the pair of them any longer.

There's a loud banging on the front door, thudding on the wood, and shaking the handles. Granny huffs and puffs, like the big bad wolf, as she slowly goes to answer the door. I squeeze past her and flop back onto the sofa. I sit down and watch. I want to say something, but I don't. I just think it.

It's Gammy Leg. He's dressed in mucky joggers and a shit-stained T-shirt, barely even able to stand. He looks smashed out of his nut, an absolute mess. Nobody was sure if he would even turn up today. The gross imbecile roars like a starving dinosaur who hasn't eaten in a long time. His injured leg trails behind him as he limps in circles around the room. He's speaking even louder than usual.

"I told her she could do one!"

"You stink of bloody booze."

"I've been speaking to them for over an hour."

Granny leans away from Gammy Leg. She shakes her head in shame and disgust. He dangles his digital pocket pad into Granny's face as though trying to hypnotize her.

"Speaking to who?"

"Monsieur – long live the great Monsieur! I've been chatting with his tech nerds. It took fucking ages to listen to all of their juicy lies. It's all coming out now."

Gammy Leg is in a world of his own.

"Will you just sit down, Gam Gam?"

Gammy Leg starts to make Granny flustered and agitated.

"They've made written claims, written fucking claims, against me. Can you believe it? They could have easily made me homeless, threatening to take the farm from me, the posh scum bags. If they had their own way, I wouldn't have had a pot to piss in."

Gammy Leg refuses to listen and continues rambling on and on. He's entirely in his own world, as though we weren't even here.

"What are you going on about?"

"He wants my farm. Keep up."

Granny seems shocked.

Pixie sheepishly tip-toes back into the room.

"Pixie! Go stick the kettle on. Get Gam Gam a strong coffee."

"Go on, babe. Make it a strong one.''

Pixie merely nods and sighs, treated like a worthless housemaid.

Me and Gammy Leg haven't seen each other since he booted me off his land. Pixie and Granny see each other more than they do the gross imbecile. He's usually drunk and working on his farm. Resentful at Granny for taking me back. Upset at Pixie for having a better relationship with his family than he does. Resentful at Lass. The family has agreed to keep me and lovely Lass apart as much as possible.

I have to stick to an agreement to stay with Granny and not end up back on the streets.

"Black, no sugar."

Pixie elegantly comes back in with the coffee.

"Stick it down, their love. No sugar?"

Pixie nods and puts the coffee on the table. Gammy Leg downs the boiling hot drink in one go, not giving two shits about it burning his gob.

"Everything alright?"

Glittering, Pixie sits back on the chair while Granny sits beside me. We're all sat down, watching Gammy Leg as though he's a paid performer. I wonder if this fat pig has this much energy when fucking Pixie. I'm surprised he hasn't broken the poor girl in half if that's the case.

“Of course, he’s not alright, daft bugger. Does he look alright?”

“I was only asking.”

Granny rolls her eyes at Pixie for asking a simple question.

“Just go get ready, Pixie-poo.”

Pixie twinkles upstairs to go get dressed.

“I’ve got digital evidence, the best kind, disproving all sorts. They’ve just cancelled my complaint, trying to say they hadn’t heard from me, even though I’ve sent about seven messages, seven!”

Gammy Leg looks like a madman, as though he genuinely thinks he will bring down a whole system, which has taken generations of patient manipulation to build up. He’s lost the plot if he believes he can do anything except rant like a daft cunt, in Granny’s front room. What the hell is he going to do with that stupid bastard leg of his. They should have chopped it off when they had the chance. Kept him in a wheelchair and pushed him off a high cliff into the murky grey sea. He drowns, and a huge shark eats his whole body, including the other leg, which still works.

Pixie comes fluttering back, fully dressed, looking like a sexy, stick-thin princess or a naked child doll. Pixie sits down in between me and Granny. I’m not going to lie, she looks pretty fit, a lot womanlier now that she's dressed. Blood starts to make its way down to my dick. Thickening it out in size as I stare at Pixie's milky soft skin. Regardless, there's only one girl for me, and that's my lovely Lass.

"We'll need to set off soon, Gam Gam. Are you coming or not?"

Asks a plain and unsympathetic Granny while chomping her lips together, picking bits of food from her mouldy and rotten front teeth, clacking like she's sucking the meat from a big bone.

"I'll give it a miss, cheers."

Gammy Leg yawns like a beast. But, of course, we mean nothing to him.

"I need a long and dirty piss!"

Gammy Leg waddles his lardy figure to the bathroom.

"Go check on him, Lad."

"Why do I have to go check on him?"

"I don't trust him up there by himself."

Fine. Anything for a peaceful life. Before I leave to go check on Gammy Leg, I watch Pixie as she goes back to her electrical poetry. She looks like an older bird now. I gawp at the pair of them before I leave. Granny looks like she's lost her marbles too. Granny says nothing. She doesn't even look up, just goes into the kitchen without saying a word. Pixie sits quietly, burying her head into her hands, guilty and ashamed of her existence. I slowly walk away and go upstairs. As I leave, my hands on the door handle, the universe sucks itself into my face, through my mouth, gasping for air like I've run out of oxygen. My spirit leaves my body through my head rather than shooting into the world. My mouth twists to the left-hand side of my face as my DNA begins to disintegrate into the walls.

HAAAWWWHHH!!!

HAAAWWWHHH!!

HAAAWWWHHH!

CHAPTER 7

Baby Boy is seated in the centre of the flat. He's wearing his sparkling pink vest top and tight pink shorts, eating out of a see-through plastic bag, and staring at the rotten, broken bath. We both still use the tub. I imagine Baby Boy daydreaming about something to do with whales or glittering fishes, enjoying the sounds of the rough ocean waves. I pull out a flask and have a cheeky sip of whisky. Me and Lass drunkenly stumble, which doesn't seem to bother Baby Boy. He's adorable. Our little kiddie-widdie is growing up so fast. It brings a tear to my eye. He loves to chase butterflies. Bless him. Every mid-afternoon, we open the window to let some in. It has to be the same-coloured butterfly. He loves yellow ones but hates red ones. We don't want to upset Baby Boy, so we try our best to attract the yellows.

We both have a few swigs out of the flask. Lass couldn't avoid taking in Baby Boy. Vanilla Streets is his mother! We all know that Vanilla Streets has an appalling reputation. She was even in contact with bands of paedophiles willing to pay months' worth of digital currency to fulfil their darkest sexual obsessions. The most requested offer Vanilla would get was to cut his taint open in front of paying customers. The sick bastards! We never saw the disgusting night walker again. Hopefully, a client stabbed Vanilla Streets to death right in the neck.

Another sip of whisky. I pass the flask to Lass.

"Baby Boy?"

No reply. Baby Boy is just sitting there. Maybe he'll eat his own skin or gobble his hand. We swig. Nobody says a word.

"Baby Boy? What are you doing?"

Baby Boy looks at us from the centre of the room. He tries to crawl toward us, but we've got his chains locked nice and tight. He can't move anywhere far from the grotty bath. Baby Boy has tried to escape quite a few times. So we needed to ensure he would stay with us in the flat.

"Just let me go."

"But it's late, Baby Boy. Very, very late."

"Please, I'm begging you, I have a family."

A couple of times, he's refused to go to bed. So we both had to devise a puppet show for him.

"Are you coming to bed, kiddo?"

"You don't have a bed! What do you want from me?"

"It's very, very late."

"I can't do this. I can't take it anymore. Just kill me."

Baby Boy breaks down. He's crying and whimpering for help. Wrapping his rusty and tightly locked chains around his body.

"Calm down, quiet, quiet, quiet."

Baby Boy does as he's told.

"How old are you again, mate?"

He doesn't answer me. He looks scared. His lip is quivering. They must be tears of joy. Shivering and shaking on the floor.

With short brown hair, glowing brown eyes, clear and pale skin, plump lips, an incredible jawline, cheekbones, a long and slender neck, and a very skinny frame, he seems way taller than he actually is. Y'know what they say about tall, skinny, white boys. They have the fattest cocks! Very skinny, pale white boys have cocks like an elephant's trunk. Also, his dress sense is kind of fucked. Patterned shirt, skinny jeans, trainers. I didn't even know idiots wore this kind of shit anymore.

"How old are you, mate?"

He still doesn't reply. Lass walks over and slaps him across the face.

"He asked how fucking old are you?"

"Err, err, err…I'm, I'm, I'm…err, err, err."

He's stuttering and mumbling a lot. Can't get his words out. He must be nervous. Nevers of joy.

"Please, please, please…no, no, no…."

He leans over and vomits all over the floor. My Baby Boy is choking, retching, and sick everywhere. It stinks.

"That's it. Just get it all up. It must be something you ate. Or a bug that's going around."

"Look, you've nothing to worry about in here. We both have your best interest at heart. Don't we, Lad?"

"Yeah, mate, we're here for you, Baby Boy. Just relax."

Baby Boy starts to calm down and stops shaking. He nods his head and gets himself together. He stops crying like a bitchy-boo-boo.

Me and Lass stand still. Our legs clenched together like we're desperately holding in a painful piss. We both stare at the little sprog in silence. No eye contact. No conversation. Nothing. We finish off the dregs of the whisky.

Baby Boy doesn't move. Just sobs and rolls himself up into a tight ball. I sluggishly grunt and drag myself into the corner. Lass runs into the hall and quickly dashes back into the room, her hands completely full. Nearly dropping the gear and tripping over her own trotters.

"Surprise! Look what I've got, babe. Better than the shit he's wearing now."

"What is it, babe?"

Lass delicately unravels a beautiful, long thobe. A long robe worn by Muslim men. The top is tailored like a shirt but is ankle-length and loose. It is white and meant to be particularly warm in winter. I have a massive grin as I imagine Baby Boy in his thobe. This will surely gain the respect of our street community.

"Baby Boy?"

"Stop it!"

Baby Boy is still acting like a cry baby. Maybe he needs us to sing him a lullaby. He needs to bloody grow up. Lass tries to help him and make things better.

"Come on, Baby Boy."

"I'm not a baby, do you hear me, you pair of nut cases. My name is not Baby Boy, you crazy cunts. Jesus! How many more times? My name is Carl. Carl! You're both psychopaths."

"Come try this on, do it for mummy."

"Fuck you."

Baby Boy spits at Lass's feet and turns away from her. His crying turns into anger.

"Come on now, this is important, Baby Boy."

The little tardo is being rude to my lovely Lass. I push myself out of the corner and over to the pair of them. How dare he speak to my sweetheart like that.

"Oi! She's talking to you. Show her some respect."

"Just stop it, just stop it, just fucking stop it. I'm not a god-damn child."

"We saved you, Baby Boy."

"No, you bloody didn't."

"Saved you from Vanilla Streets."

"There is no Vanilla Streets, you pair of lunatics."

"She would have sold you for peanuts if we didn't take you in. Vanilla would have had your taint cut open and fucked."

"You dragged me off the streets, cut me with razor blades, made me sniff your drugs. I swear on my kids' lives. I'll have you begging for mercy, begging for your…."

"It's about time others felt the pain we've been through. Do you think we've had easy lives? We've had the hardest lives. Baby Boy, in his posh boy city life, try growing up on the land, you little prick. You wouldn't last five minutes."

Lass drops the thobe and quickly lunges at Baby Boy. She grabs him by the scruff of his neck and drags him to the ground. She gets on top and wraps her legs around his body. Baby Boy kicks and screams, but the thick, heavy chains keep him from moving. She puts both hands around Baby Boys' neck and rattles his head. It smashes against the hard floor. Lass lets go of his neck and starts to smack his stupid face.

Blood splatters everywhere!

Blood squirting! Blood on his face! Blood all over her hands! Blood on her face!

Blood and guts! Blood and guts! Blood and guts! Blood and guts! Blood and guts!

I look down, and he's lying in a dark red pool of thick blood. He's swimming in rivers of blood, drenched the entire floor and soaking through the floorboards. The blood dribbles out of his neck and splatters over his face.

Blood and guts! Blood and guts! Blood and guts! Blood and guts! Blood and guts!

He's dead.

Lass has killed him. Baby Boy is dead in her arms.

Lass looks at me. She looks down at Baby Boy's dead body. We take a minute to mourn the loss of Baby Boy. Then, we stand above his body and gaze at it with wonder.

Lass shakes her head in disgust.

"I'm just going to cut his taint open, babe."

"That's a good idea."

"Rest in peace, Baby Boy. This evil cunt Carl took you from us."

I walk past Lass, lean over Carl's dead body, and grab his lifeless hand. Dripping in blood, definitely no pulse or heartbeat. I inspect his rotting fingers, one by one, until I can force off his wedding ring. I step over Carl's body and move over to Lass.

"This is for you."

I hand my sweetheart Carl's ring.

"Aww. You're so romantic."

Me and Lass share a long kiss.

The ring is too big for her long and slender fingers. Fuck you, Carl! I kick Carl in his ribs as hard as I can. Lass spits on his bloodied face. Regardless, Lass puts the ring on her wedding finger.

We share another long kiss.

I go over to the other side of the flat and pick up my razor blade. I pass my razor blade to Lass.

"Thanks, babe."

"Let's slash his taint open, shall we?"

"You're so creative."

"I love you."

"I love you too."

"Want to know something?"

"What?"

"You look sexy covered in blood."

Hours later. Coming out of our most extended drug binge to date. Me and Lass are lying on the floor. Empty bags of purple cri-cringle-brekk cover the entirety of the flat. I stroke lovely Lass's hair with my hand. It feels so soft. Like fresh feathers plucked out of a plumped pillow. We're out of drugs and booze. Hunger starts to really kick in.

We've been silent for a long time. Admiring the beauty of our flat and gratitude that we have each other. Experiencing true love. I love her so much, it hurts. I hope she loves me this much. I hope she does. Me and Lass get the shakes as we start to come down from the purple. I start up a little food game to change the mood. The reality of having none of the purple dust or a little sippy-roo-roo really starts to agitate us. Hunger kicks in like never before.

"If you could have anything right now, what would it be?"

"Food?"

"Yeah, one meal, anything you like."

"Does it have to be a meal or anything I want?"

"Mix and match."

"Chips, with salt."

"That's your one meal? Fucking hell, what a load of shit."

"Yeah, well, it's my fantasy."

"Fair enough."

My own game starts to make me really flipping hungry.

"Looks like we're starving."

"Probably."

"I'll tell you what we have got, can't believe I forgot about this, it's a good un! You're going to be excited. Get your excited face ready."

I sprint into the hall, leaving Lass to lie on the floor without me. I'm sad that she didn't ask me what my one meal would be. I dash back into the flat, hiding something behind my back. It's a surprise. Surprise! Surprise! Surprise! Surprise!

"We do have some scrin-scranny-scroo! You've got two guesses."

"Just tell me. I can't be bothered with any more of your games."

I pull a big tin of tomato soup from behind my back. The can has a big dint down the middle and a crack on each side.

"Surprise!"

"Urgh! Soup?"

"Yeah, babe"

"You're useless. Let's see it then."

Useless is a bit harsh, considering I've produced something that will likely keep us from dying of starvation. I hand the soup to Lass.

"Tommy soup?"

"I risked my neck for that bastard. You're welcome."

"This is all we have?"

"Yep."

"Fine. If this is our only option. It's hardly a sippy-roo-roo, or a line of the finest purple, but let's do it."

"Cold."

"I'm not eating cold soup. I'm not that desperate."

"Odds?"

"I'm not playing."

"When you've been odds, you've got to say?"

"Nah."

"That's your bloody rule, babe, so jog on. Odds?"

"Alright then, fifty to one."

"Bandit.

"What?"

"Give us better odds than that."

"Hang on, what's the question?"

"Odds on, you and me, so I'll be doing it too, you and me, eating this cold soup."

"Ten to one."

"Five to one"

"Fine."

Lass has given in. She's finally playing a game of odds with me. We've not played odds long time. We have a lot of beautiful and unique memories of playing that game.

"Stand up. If you're going to do it, do it properly."

You need to always stand up to play odds. That was Lass's rule when she invented the game. So Lass stands up as I put the soup in the middle of the room.

"Feeling ready, feeling warmed up?"

"Just get on with it."

She's so moody. I get it, we're out of stash and sip, but I've got us tommy soup, the ungrateful little bitch.

"After three, babe.

"Three."

"Two.

"One."

"Four!"

We both said four! Champion! Champion! Champion!

"Ha! Beat you at your own game."

"I don't care, you boring twat, just crack it open."

I open the tin of soup. We both have to down the can.

"Get your laughing gear around that."

I grab the tin of soup from the middle of the flat. I crack it open using the cap on the top before passing the soup to a moody Lass.

"Why do I have to go first?"

"It's your odds, love. Get that down you."

Me and Lass both share the cold tin of soup. We pass between each other as though we're drinking a can of the finest alcoholic oil or sharing a doobie. We use it playfully, chasing each other around the room, wiping it all over each other. All over our hands, each other's faces, in our hair. We hold hands and share a soft and intimate moment. I give Lass a kiss on both cheeks. She gives me one on the lips.

"What about, you know, Carl?"

I inspect Carl's disgusting body. He's near the stinky bathtub. The smell makes us feel sick, the buzzing flies begin to annoy us, and having to look at his gross face is rank.

"We can stick him on the pile in the hall, on top of the other dead bodies."

We sit down and drink the remains of the soup. Neither of us says a word.

HAAAWWWHHH!!!

HAAAWWWHHH!!

HAAAWWWHHH!

CHAPTER 8

My arms are banging against the sides of this big white machine. I hold tightly onto the metal bars as I hear a switch from above my head. The mat I'm lying on is electronically pulled forward, and I'm free to leave the machine. Bright lights shine like the sun into my gormless face. I cover my blinkers with my hands. My fingers stink of shit. I feel safe in the darkness with my eyes closed. I'd rather sniff shit in the dark than have lights glaring into my mush, with the sound of tools blasting into my ears. I begin to see the lights dim down through my fingers. I decide to bite the bullet and look. Everything is white. White walls, white bed, white machine, white ceiling. We get it, we get it, we get it, this place likes white. In every corner of the room, there are cameras. I look around the room, at the machine, over both of my shoulders, to my sides. The room appears to be empty. I turn my body and lean over to my left, leaving the bed.

I stand up, but my arms are taped up, and my head is in agony. Especially my scar. My scar appears to be bastard bleeding! I quickly rip the tape wrapped around my wrists and arms like plastic handcuffs. I pull some of the bed-sheet paper and hold it to my scar. I soak up all the blood running through my hair and down my back. I walk to the door and try the handle with my left hand. The right hand is doing an excellent job of soaking up the blood. I walk out of the room and into the hall. I look left, but nobody. I look right, nobody. I slowly turn and see orange writing on the door. It reads room forty-three.

The tissue has managed to soak up most of my bleeding. I roll it up and chuck it down on the floor. It's probably best not to touch or poke the scar. My body is aching, so I drag my lifeless legs down the white halls. There are more rooms with blacked-out windows and orange writing on the doors. Each one with numbers written on it. Forty-two, forty-one, forty, etc. I make it to room thirty-five, which seems to be the last down this corridor. Eight rooms? I wonder where the other thirty-four are? I try the door handles of each room, but all are locked except forty-three. I'm locked in from both ends of the halls and can't unlock any other room. I stroll back into forty-three, as it's pointless trying to leave. I sit on the edge of the bed and stare at the vast machine. Its flashing red dots from an enormous projector above hang from the ceiling. I notice a small window. I stand up and trip over a fucking cable. Idiots.

I walk over, lean down as much as possible, and look out this small window. There's this massive truck. Driving through this mighty fence into a courtyard. The courtyard is surrounded by metal, covered in barbed wire and sharp spikes. Way too high for anybody to even attempt climbing over. Even if, by some magic, a person or group did manage to climb this extravagant fence, they would either fall and break their necks or smash their heads. Or catch themselves on the sharp spikes and get pierced wide open, guts splattered everywhere. Or be captured on one of the hundred cameras, seen, and struck down.

If none of that happens, I'm confident the whole fence will be electrified. That would probably take you down. The guards let this big truck in through the gate, a truck that could be mistaken for a train. In bright orange letters, it says 'Monsieur Corporations', as does everything in this place. I intensely gawp through the glass, as three built blokes, in black uniforms park up and unlock the very secure train-like truck. My jaw slowly drops to the floor, my gob wide open. I see what look like prisoners, young prisoners, very young prisoners, being herded like cattle from the truck, across the courtyard and into the building opposite. There are roughly fifty men and boys, handcuffed and prodded, one after another, after another, after another. My heart starts to beat exceptionally fast, I gasp for air, and I feel like I might have a heart attack or that my brain will splatter out of my head. I limp as quickly as possible from the window to the door. The top of my head is still in agony. I reach the door when two massive cunts in black uniforms walk in. Bald and built like brick shit houses. They look exactly like the guys herding the cattle outside. Got to be about six-foot-three or six-foot-four. I decide to keep my mush shut.

"Come on then, young un, let's be having you."

"Which room are we taking him to?"

"We're taking him to Room Zero."

The thinner of the two smiles and pats the fatter one on his back.

"How will we get him down four flights of stairs?"

"Will do you some good, fat boy."

The thinner one grins. The fatter one sighs.

"You'll be a good boy and walk without any hassle, won't you?"

"They'll be no trouble from me, boys."

I casually reassure them they won't have to use violence or anything against me. I'll behave myself and do as I say. I don't have much of a choice.

"See! The young un has agreed to be a good boy."

The thinner one nods at me and gives me a cheeky wink. Fatty is still annoyed that we've got to treck down four flights of stairs. He clearly can't hack it. The three of us walk out of the room with me in front. The next thing I know, I'm being guided through a small office, away from all the other numbered rooms, through various corridors, and into a room with a giant zero on the door. Me and the two big bastards haven't said a word to each other. Just the fatty taking big deep breaths, the thinner one laughing at him, and me trying to stop myself from having a panic attack and passing out from the pain in my head. They both lead me to Room Zero and onto the bed.

"Wait here, young un."

They speak and rabble over each other, telling me not to move, like a slapstick double act.

"There will be somebody to see to you soon."

The circus double act leaves me to it. I'm just here. Alone. There are no big machines, tools, windows, no fancy shit like the rooms upstairs. That's what makes Room Zero so infamous and different. It's just me, a bed, and an empty room.

It feels like I've been in Room Zero for weeks. I'm not allowed to leave and can only have people come into the room. When I've attempted to walk out, they have their big burly bastards drag me back in. Now I'm like a grey squirrel high up in a tree, scavenging for nuts, shooting my head toward the door handle, and freezing in a trance-like state. These assholes bring me food and then lock my door. A special soup that tastes like piss. I don't want these dickheads near me. They want to come in and talk to me, drag me places where I don't want to go and do things to me that I don't want to do. I'd go as far as saying that I hate them. These are people who I would happily punch in the face and spit on. That's the thing with this centre, there's always somebody watching you. There are more cameras than I've had erections.

This centre is where selected males are taken for private experimentation. We're cleared of all previous memories using new state-funded technology. We have our past identities taken away from us. We have our visions for the future exterminated. The selected males are injected, with testosterone and other hormones, to discover the inner workings of our minds. This centre exists to dig into our previous lives and past crimes.

We're all hooked up to the exact same system at all times. Nothing outside of the online tracked grid exists. If anything new tries to form, it will be destroyed. This centre will never let us know where we came from. We're just here to be tested on. They use their implanted brain chips alongside other sciences and medicines. Henceforth, everything we're allowed to see, hear, and smell will be specifically designed using these implants. I'm sitting on my bed and glaring at the door. The centre has allowed images to fly around in my head for what feels like a lifetime. The pictures which spread around the mind are far more critical than this shit hole. No matter what science and technology fucking tells us.

We're nothing more than this centre's bitch boys, who were all sold like slaves to punish us for past crimes. Our experiments have allegedly proven that all men are born into a sick and twisted mindset. Ha! What a joke. They genuinely think what they do to us is the height of compassion. Everybody knows that compassion isn't genuine. Top doctors and scientists have told me that man is pre-determined to be a criminal. Science and technology don't have to change. 'Monsieur Corporations' needs to double down on monitoring our everyday lives. Apparently, we aren't fit to be released back into society.

Since they last wiped my memory, using their cunty-wunty brain chip, they have told me some crazy shit. Sometimes they don't wipe us. Most times, they do. I can't keep up with my own wipes. Whatever benefits the all-mighty tech giants at 'Monsieur Corporations'. This place is now the world's foremost lab testing facility. Thanks to its criminal slaves, it has succeeded in its goal of taking apart the brains of young male lab rats.

My head feels absolutely fucked. Both inside and outside. I don't know anything about my past. The way this place treats me, it's as though I never existed outside of here. I'm spoken to as merely a statistical measurement of analysis. I don't know what awaits me from this point forward. I'm among many who have encouraged a lot of support from various donors toward the centre's enforced approach.

The rattling of tools outside my room soon turns into an abrupt entrance through the door. My instincts tell me to jump onto the bed and scream at the cunts! But that doesn't seem to work in this place. It only leads to violence and more injections. Long periods of isolation. They nod at me. I nod back at them. I lift myself out of bed and walk over. They smile, and I smile. I've got no energy to have a fight. In their eyes, science cannot be wrong. Corporations would not lie. Data and measurements are all that there is. We are scum, and they are Gods. Their technological trials have worked. 'Monsieur Corporations' can now take credit. We're born evil, we're born criminals, and we're born to be punished. It's in the male DNA, in the male genetics, it's in the male medically induced brain chips.

Two guards and the top female doctor drag me into a bright room. I'm shocked to see other patients in the room. All dressed like me in gowns. All waiting. I wonder what they're waiting for. Why have I never seen these people before? They've done a great job at keeping us apart. So many questions and thoughts. Waves of fear and anxiety are racing through me.

"It's great to finally have you all together."

Top Fem Doc plods to the centre of the room. She poses and tells everybody she's the most powerful woman around this dump.

"If you could all join me in a circle, that would be fabulous."

Myself and four other delinquents culminate in a circle, with Top Fem Doc at the centre. We all look on with indifference and confusion.

"It's great to have some of you here."

Everybody nervously scans the brightly lit room to understand their fellow freaks. Who were my damaged and depraved comrades? As soon as we quickly catch sight of each other, we all nervously and, in unison, direct our eyes back toward the slippery floor. All nearly falling over our own feet as we skid back and forth. Everybody looks extremely tired and lacking in energy. We all look away and avoid making eye contact.

Top Fem Doc scowls and stays silent. She goes through some notes, realising that she has to be somewhere or has forgotten something. She storms out of the room while a nurse comes in and sits down to watch over us like we're a group of toddlers. Nurse pays no attention to us as she flicks her way through her digital pocket pad. We all continue to nervously look at the ground. None of us want to make friends. We just want to leave. But there's probably more chance of changing the sky's colour than making sense of this bastard place. Manipulating us into thinking and feeling exactly what they want us to. Playing tricks with our minds and trying to reprogramme our brains.

Top Fem Doc eventually returns.

"Did they play nicely, Nursey?"

Nurse simply nods.

"Great! Remember, you're all sick individuals and need our help. Don't you? That's why we've waited such a long time to get you all together. You're all implanted now, so everything should be fine going forward."

We stand and watch as Top Fem Doc babbles on and on. She continues blurting out some crazy shit. I start to feel a queasy sensation deep down in my belly. I turn away from the circle and try to take deep breaths. I hope that the déjà vu passes. I can just about hear what Top Fem Doc is saying behind me. Nurse sounds like she's mumbling too. It's as though she's speaking directly into my ear. My queasy begins to subside. Nobody seems to have noticed that I've turned away into my own little world. As I turn back around toward the circle, Top Fem Doc has stopped ranting. Images begin to pop into my head. Fast ideas and quick visions of families. Lots of families and relationships. These blurry mind photos zoom by one after another, after another, after another. I start to see the darkness and fuzz more clearly. The patient next to me drops down to the floor. His legs shake violently, his eyes roll back, his mouth twists to one side, arms fly above his head. He starts to screech and spasm. Making horrifically loud noises.

HAAAWWWHHH!!!
HAAAWWWHHH!!
HAAAWWWHHH!

CHAPTER 9

I swagger up to Chip Fat Mam's door and bang on it loudly. Almost punching it with my knuckles. Nobody answers, so I thud even louder. I use both of my mitts to bang.

My knock gets louder and louder.

"Alright, I'm coming!"

Chip Fat Mam slowly opens the door. I'm standing there with my arms folded. My gormless mother looks as though she's seen a ghost. Neither of us says a word.

The best physical description of Chip Fat Mam is that of a greasy tennis ball. Very small, very round, dripping in grease. Carrying weight in all the wrong places. Shoulder-length brown hair never washed or dried, ickle-wickle facial features, flabby three chins, an incredibly round father Christmas belly. You can tell just from looking that Chip Fat Mam and Gammy Leg are related. Chip Fat Mam doesn't look after her health.

"Can I come in?"

I eventually break the unbearable silence between the two of us. Just staring like a couple of children. She seems genuinely shocked, unsure if we would ever see each other again. My mother suffers from a mild form of autism. Her noticeable signs are minimal speech, easily confused, very anxious, scared, and highly agreeable. Her confidence is very low, and she is easily manipulated. She mostly starts her sentences by repeating the last thing somebody else said. She doesn't understand a joke, a bit of banter, or any questions or rational facts in any deep or meaningful way. Everything is very surface level.

"Can you come in? Err, err, yeah, you can come in."

Chip Fat Mam awkwardly lets me into her front room, closing the door behind us.

I confidently bounce about, carrying my bag. I'm calmly showing more of an old masculinity and confidence. The only place a male can learn how to become a man nowadays is within the confines of his own mind. Today's world will turn you into a mess if you let it. I'm no longer a scared and chubby soft boy. But a strong and confident man. Mother looks down at her fluffy red carpet. This is likely to be caused by her nerves and anxiety. I stare at her, tilting my head to one side to glare.

"Come here then, give us a hug!"

I walk over to Chip Fat Mam and wrap my arms around her neck. We have a big hug until she slowly pulls away. Chip Fat Mam awkwardly smiles. She used to shag anybody who would ask her. Hence why Short Ass keeps her under such strict lock and key. She doesn't know how to show emotion or love, especially to those close to her. She is very socially awkward and struggles to understand other people. If Short Ass told her to jump off a bridge tomorrow, she would do it.

"You're looking well, Mother."

"You're looking well? Err, err, yeah, you're looking well too."

Chip Fat Mam nervously chokes on her words. I feel sorry for her. Her condition seems to have got worse. It's definitely still the woman who abandoned me. I'm annoyed at myself for having sadness for a woman who never loved or supported us.

"You wanted to see the state of me last year. So both Gammy Leg and Granny kicked me out onto the street."

Chip Fat Mam bluntly grunts like a pig before looking at the carpet.

"Nice gaff."

"Nice gaff? Err, err, yeah, it is a nice gaff."

"Nice 3D virtual touch screen."

"3D virtual touch screen? Err, err, yeah. Short Ass wants us to get one of those new ones that fill the wall."

"Oh, I bet he does."

Chip Fat Mam lives in a small cottage on the land. This is a relatively comfortable and safe area. Two bedrooms, pretty nice gaff, away from all of the posh twats immigrating from the city, similar to that of Gammy Leg's farm.

"Err, err, yeah, what do you want?"

"Hmm. How do I say this? This is rude of me, just turning up like this."

Chip Fat Mam is very unsure of what to say. She's embarrassed I'm here and lacks the words or social skills to express anything. She just shakes her head at me. Hinting that I can't stay there. I don't want to stay! I'm here to take Lass. I just quietly nod along. She seemed proud of herself that she put her foot down by insisting, awkwardly, that I couldn't stay. I scout about the room and spring around like an animal. Then, things start to heat up and become very tense. Chip Fat Mam becomes even more nervous. Unsure of what I want or what I might do. It's been such a long time since she's seen me that she has no idea who I am.

"Turning up like this? Err, err, yeah, you can stay, only for a few hours."

"Cheers, mother."

"Cheers. Err, err, yeah. Want a juice?"

"Go on then. I'll have little a juicey-wucey."

Chip Fat Mam waddles into the kitchen to make me a drink of juicey-wucey. I prowl around the room like a tiger on the hunt, touching and feeling anything in sight, brushing my hands along the black leather furniture as though I'm looking for something. It's tranquil. The only noise I can hear is a bird tweeting. I move over to the window and see nothing but trees and plants. I pick up a photo of Chip Fat Mam and Short Ass which sits above the fireplace. I breeze toward the massive 3D virtual touch screen attached to the wall above the sofa. I stare with disgust at this photo for quite some time. I chuck the photo down, back above the fireplace. I don't care if it's upside down or the glass has smashed. I grab my bag and head for the door. I've made a massive mistake being in a room with this evil cow. I'll get Lass some other way. As I head for the door Chip Fat Mam plops back into the room with two glasses of juicey-wucey. I turn around and grab my drink.

"Cheers, Mother."

"Cheers. Err, err, yeah, sit down."

We both sit at opposite ends of her fancy glass table.

"You've got it all sussed out by the looks of it?"

Chip Fat Mam finds my banter ridiculous and looks at the stainless red carpet.

"You've landed on your feet."

I'm sat in Short Ass's place. We sit in silence. I nod along politely to the silence. I'm such an idiot. I can't stop thinking about how Chip Fat Mam told me I'm only welcome to stay for a few hours. I twist and turn in my seat, sporadically drinking big gulps of my rank drink. Her controlling boyfriend, Short Ass, is tiny, four-foot-eleven, and suffers from little man syndrome. More like little dick syndrome. Tiny hands, small feet, small mouth. He clearly needs to dominate those who are weaker. He needs to feel superior and cleanse himself of his small stature insecurities. His hair is thinning and grey, he's in reasonably good shape for his age, and he proudly sticks to the green agenda diet plan. Virtue signalling, so everybody in the area thinks he's cock of the walk. None of that matters when he's alone at three in the morning, taking that early morning piss. He looks down and sees a tiny penis that never made a baby. Eat all the greens you want, Short Ass. You've not got anything to show for it where it truly matters.

"It's funny, mother, how everybody around you starts to die when you get older. Your own life becomes like a ticking time bomb."

I want some kind of feeling, some kind of emotion out of her.

"Life. Err, err, yeah, life."

Chip Fat Mam uses a one-word answer, not understanding the depth or philosophy behind my simple point. I'm really trying my fucking best to hold in my own frustrations at how utterly stupid and unaware my mother truly is. It's like talking to a teenager who hasn't lived or seen anything. She simply nods and agrees.

"An old mate from school killed himself the other week. Yep. I saw it online. He chucked himself off a bridge in the city. Everybody filmed it and found it hilarious."

"A bridge? Err, err, yeah, bridge."

"He was called One Arm Bandit. Yeah, because he had a robotic arm. It's weird because I had a dream about him when I was at Granny's."

Chip Fat Mam wriggles in her seat and can still not look me in the eye. I jump up from the table and start to dominate the front room. Me and Lass were always more intelligent than Chip Fat Mam, even from a very young age. We could read, write, spell, and count much better than our mother.

"I had this dream. I was walking with you, and I was eight years old. One Arm Bandit was working. Doing his evening shift. Then he came outside to have a smoke as me, and you were walking past. He starts to flirt with you, and it's working. I beg you to hurry up because we're coming to see Lass. In the dream, you had promised me for months and months that we could go see Lass. Then One Arm Bandit whips his dick out, and you start sucking it! It went on for ages. I'm crying for you to hurry up. Then you pull his dick out of your mouth, and he spunks in my eye. The bastard. How messed up is that, though? Then I hear online that One Arm Bandit is dead. Do you want to know what you told me the last time we saw each other? You said, slurred more like, you couldn't believe your son, who you had tried to bring up on your own, had turned out like this."

I'm quietly raging by this point. Trying my best to hold everything in. I'm really struggling. The atmosphere changes. I drift over to the photograph of Chip Fat Mam and Short Ass. I slowly pick it up. This mild autism doesn't bother Short Ass. He really loves the power that he has over her. He gets to have all of the intellectual and moral authority. Not to mention the dark kick he gets from Chip Fat Mam's childlike behaviour. He gets to fulfil his sexual fantasies of dominating and controlling a child but without actually having to go down that dark path.

"You really have carved out a nice little life for yourself."

"Nice life. Err, err, yeah, nothing special."

"Very special."

"I keep having another dream. I'm lying on the floor of an empty room, it's more of a flat than a room, but it has no furniture. I'm just waking up from my afternoon nap. I've been working hard all morning and just finished my shift. Helping to clean up the blackened streets. I noticed somebody must have forced their way into the flat while I was conked out. Doesn't exactly take much to get in. But I don't think it was two people. It was just one. They've been watching the flat for days, maybe even weeks. They've worked out my daily routine, writing it down and memorising it from the moment I wake up to the second I go to sleep."

I start to walk in circles around the room and dominate my surroundings.

"I get back from work earlier than usual, so the Robber-Scum-Fuck wasn't expecting anybody to be here. They must have seen me asleep on the floor and realised I could have woken up any second. Robber-Scum-Fuck… ass licking…slut bucket…shit skull...must have seen me asleep on the floor and tried to move my body. Robber-Scum-Fuck was trying to grab my Glock from the floorboards and keep it for themselves. But it didn't go to plan. They couldn't get under the floorboard because I was lying on it. Robber-Scum-Fuck got frustrated, nervous, and scared 'what if I get caught?' he kept saying. Their mind gets the better of them. Robber-Scum-Fuck crawls up and runs out of the flat. I could wake up any minute, and there could be a fight. If I wake up while he's still here, I could grab my Glock and blow his brains out."

Chip Fat Mam nervously looks up and down, up and down, up and down.

"Robber-Scum-Fuck goes back to his gang on the street. All his mates laugh and point at what a worthless piece of shit he is. There are at least five of them. Ha! Couldn't even get a flat from a tired man who had passed out on his own floor.

They all punch him in the head and face, and he drops to the ground. They kick his ribs and limbs, drag his lifeless body down an alley and stick long, sharp objects up his tight asshole. That's what he gets for coming back with nothing. Everyone else in the gang has all got gold and silver from their jobs."

I breeze around the room and run my fingers across everything in sight. Chip Fat Mam hasn't got the nerve to say anything. I could rob the gaff clean if I wanted. But, out of respect for Lass, I won't. But I could.

"Robber-Scum-Fuck is kicked out of the gang. Nowhere to go. He slowly limps to one of the old broken-down churches. There's still enough there to be able to climb up onto the fucked-up Church roof. He decides to climb up. Using whatever energy he has left. Robber-Scum-Fuck attempts to climb up the side of the Church. He misses his step. Shit! Nearly falls. It reminds him of what a useless cretin he is. He probably won't even be able to get himself up onto the roof. He climbs down and decides to carry on living. Prove himself to the world. Maybe even start training to do morning clean-ups, like myself."

I sit back down at the head of the table. Leaning forward on the wood and staring at Chip Fat Mam. Now I'm genuinely head of this house.

"In the dream, I sit on the floor of my flat and think about Robber-Scum-Fuck. He needs a friend. A true friend. Somebody that will love him no matter what. Family. That's what he needs. True love. Tight family. From the bottom of my heart, I wish Robber-Scum-Fuck well. I really hope he puts themselves together. I start to tear up. Jesus! Mother, I'm crying, ha! I'm fucking crying, Mother, Jesus! Look at me. I'm a Nancy boy. That's would Gammy Leg would call me for crying. A little Nancy boy faggot. Only girls cry. Girls and faggots. You cry when you have your period or get fucked up the Ass. That's it. Only those two times. That's what Gammy Leg used to say. I never saw him cry. Never."

Chip Fat Mam's face goes bright red. She wriggles in her seat but doesn't show emotion other than being uncomfortable and awkward.

"Mother, I've never met another man in our family who showed emotion. They've only screamed, shouted, roared, barked, hit, struck, punched, smacked, smashed, demolished, wrecked, and destroyed. Am I right?"

She avoids eye contact at all costs. This bitch is going to hear my incredible dream. Worship the vision of the chosen son. I press forward and perform at the table.

"I feel so sad for Robber-Scum-Fuck. I can relate to being that much of a joke. I wish that he had completed his mission. That he took my Glock and killed me. I wish Robber-Scum-Fuck took my flat for the gang. He should have made his way in the world. I tell myself that if I ever find out what he looks like and if I bump into him, I'll be his friend. He can come around to the empty flat. We can get smashed up and look at the starry night through the flat window."

Chip Fat Mam stares at the door. I can tell she's hoping I leave soon. But I ain't going anywhere. She's hearing the rest of my dream.

"I've made up my mind about Robber-Scum-Fuck. I lie down on the floor in my empty flat. I stare out and wait for the night sky. When I befriend Robber-Scum-Fuck, I'll share all of my gold and silver with him. In the dream, that's what they pay me. I've got all the gold and silver anybody needs. Then, when the nuclear apocalypse happens, we'll have jars, tins, gold, silver, tablets, and each other. Fuck this! I jump up from the bare floor. I ain't waiting any longer. He's outside by himself. He needs me. That's how much of a good person I am. Always helping the needy. Cleaning up the streets and working with special enforcers to combat crime."

Short Ass comes swaggering through the front door. A tiny man's swagger. He looks like an injured penguin shagged by a polar bear.

"I forgot my flipping pocket pad."

"Short Ass! I was just telling a story about you."

"About me?"

"Yeah, just let me finish it quickly."

Short Ass stands in the room doorway as we have a very tense stare down. I continue regardless, and he doesn't try to stop me.

"I'm on my feet, and it's hours later. I quickly grab my Glock. Have I got enough bullets? I have. That's a good job. You can't do these things without many bullets to get you through. I load my Glock and go to save Robber-Scum-Fuck. I say, 'I'm coming to help you! I'm coming to save you!' I run around the blackened streets until I find him. Guess what? It's amazing. It's you, Short Ass. You're the Robber-Scum-Fuck. You're sat on a curb in a curled-up mess. I go to touch you, and you reveal your face. I'm shocked. You begin to laugh. You point and start teasing me. It was all fake! You've tricked me into leaving the flat to come and recuse you. It's a trap. Your gang raided my place while I was away. They now live there, and I'm the one who has nothing. Then I woke up. That's the end of my dream."

Silence. Even more silence. Long live silence.

"Can I have a quick word in the kitchen?"

"It's fine, you two love birds. I need to use the bog anyway. Where is it?"

I insist that the two twats can talk about me while I have a slash.

"Upstairs, first left."

I open the door, close it behind me, sit on the bottom step, and listen to the pair of cretins slag me off.

"What's going on?'"

"What's going on? Err, err, yeah, what is going on?"

"What have you done this time, idiot?"

Short Ass sounds disgusted that I'm here. He sounds even more resentful toward Chip Fat Mam for letting me in.

"I told him. Err, err, yeah. I told him that he could, I told him. Err, err, yeah, I told him that he could…."

"You better get your son out of here. I'll talk with him, but I'm not happy about it."

I'm only here for Lass anyway. Once she gets back, we're off! I swagger into the front room, smirking and wagging my finger in approval.

"Now that's what I call a flipping bath. Eco-friendly, I'm assuming? Sure as hell looks like it?"

Short Ass is highly uncomfortable with my presence.

"How long have you two been together again? Remind me, it's been a very long time."

I float around the gaff like stepping on a cloud, touching everything. I want Short Ass to snap at me so that I can take Lass and leave the land. I could hit him or hit both of them. I could go out into the streets and hit everybody that I see. That would be so much fun.

"Does she ever mention me?"

I aggressively point at Chip Fat Mam.

"Not really."

Short Ass looks directly into my eyes with piercing daggers. I'll fucking hurt him with my fists, cut open his neck, drink his blood. But, instead, I stare back, knowing that my smirk and cheek annoy him. I'm the ultimate provocateur! Short Ass can suck my cheesy dick and lick my unwiped asshole.

"Cool, mate."

I shrug off Short Asses' insult. He takes his seat at the head of the table.

"Err, err, yeah, yeah, drink?"

A nervous Chip Fat Mam tries to break the ice with liquid offerings.

"I'm fine!"

A moody Short Ass snaps back.

"I'm fine too, mother."

Me and Short Ass aren't breaking eye contact. As a result, the atmosphere becomes very intense.

"Don't you have to get off to work, Short Ass?"

There's evident tension between me and Short Ass. A game of who can hold it together the longest. Short Ass seems to be winning. He's starting to get to me, ignoring my questions or throwing them away with pointless answers.

"Lad, your life can't be that hard?"

Short Ass mocks me from the head of the table, assuming that he knows about my life, he offers the bait, and I can't help but take it.

"Can't be that hard. Are you fucking kidding me? Nobody to turn to, nobody to talk to, always having to watch my back, the only girl I've ever loved I'm not allowed to see?"

"What do you want? Just say your final piece and leave."

Short Ass tries to stay calm. Chip Fat Mam doesn't say a single word. I've had enough of the pair of them. I'm getting my Lass and leaving.

"I've had no one, but you two weren't interested. So you've been out here living the good life with your lovely house, 3D virtual bollocks, and eco-friendly-toilet. Didn't even attempt to check if I was alright. But you both managed to keep me and Lass apart."

"Can you tell him to leave?"

Chip Fat Mam doesn't respond but merely looks at the carpet.

"You two deserve each other, no thought for anybody else but yourselves. I'm not going anywhere."

Short Ass stands up to confront me, face to face, man to man.

"What does your mother owe you exactly? Probably never worked a day in your life, already trying to ruin other people's lives and make demands of them."

Me and Short Ass are practically nose to nose. A fight could easily break out, both trying to dominate and win. I try to remember why I'm here.

"Mrs High and Mighty over there!"

I point to Chip Fat Mam, who continues to ignore me.

"I've worked hard for this life, so if you think you can come and shake things up, you can think again. Because we aren't letting that happen, and Lass isn't coming with you."

"Maybe I could have worked and had a good life, but my life is pretty much done now."

"Get the violins out."

Short Ass is practically laughing in my face.

"Err, err, just leave, please."

Chip Fat Mam finally looks at me and asks me to leave her house.

"Leave now while you still can."

Short Ass would absolutely love it if I made the first move. Then, he could claim self-defence and even send me to one of those behavioural camps or testing clinics.

"Is that a threat, Short Ass?"

"Yeah, it is."

"Threat? Err, err, yeah, no, it isn't."

"I understand everything that's gone on. I get what's happening now, and I definitely know what will happen if this idiot son of yours doesn't piss off out of my house."

Short Ass is very calm and composed. I can tell that he's given his actions some thought. He's trying to get a violent rise to finally turn Lass against me.

"If you don't walk out of my door, you'll live to regret it."

Chip Fat Mam wants me to leave for the sake of her relationship. I pick up my bag and walk out of the gaff. I accept that things can never be fixed with my mother. But I'll definitely be back to get Lass, whatever it takes.

HAAAWWWHHH!!!

HAAAWWWHHH!!

HAAAWWWHHH!

CHAPTER 10

I'm sitting on my wooden stool and stare up at him like a young un saying his first words for Mummy and Daddy. My own little naughty step. The legs on my naughty step start to wobble. They could break any second. That's the last time I let these cunts choose what I sit on. I prefer a naughty plastic step, not like this piece of shit.

"I had no choice, doctor. He came at me first, the prick. I was just defending myself."

"Defending yourself from what?"

"That cretin!"

"Err, let me speak to my colleague for a minute."

"No worries."

The doctor leaves me sitting in the naughty room. Closing the door behind him. I used to hate this clinic back in the day. But I know in my heart that they will understand what I did. Self-defence to save my own life.

The doctor walks back into the naughty room. He's already here to help me.

"Have you had a medical check up recently?"

"No, mate, not in a long time."

"Right, OK. That explains a lot."

"Can you tell I don't need one? I'm fresh as a fucking daisy."

"I've spoken with my colleagues, and we all think you should come with us for a medical examination."

"I've told you, doctor, I don't need a medical examination."

"Sir…"

"Don't call me sir! Sorry, I'm sorry, it just brings back horrible nightmares when I hear the name, sir. Horrific nightmares."

"We all strongly believe that it will be in everybody's best interest, especially yours, to come with us for one of our medical examinations."

"I told you, I don't need one."

"It's clear to us that you do need one."

"Why? Because I was defending myself."

"We understand your mental health is important, especially in this clinic. However, if left unaddressed, it can lead to a breakdown, or worse."

"It was self-defence, for fucks sake, mate. My life was in danger."

I stand up and lightly tap my broken naughty step. The little legs come off, and it falls to the floor. I knew it would. Everything in this place needs redoing.

"Self defence against who?"

"That evil twat who kept coming into my room when I was in group sessions. What kind of a man would steal from another man. That's pure scum of the earth."

"Who are you talking about?"

"In my room, in the corner, underneath the bag. I had to hide the body. I had no choice but to wrap the body in black bags. Mainly to hide the face. I couldn't look at the face, not with all those stab marks. And his neck, fuck me, mate. More blood pouring from his neck than a bird's vag giving birth to triplets."

"Are you sure about this?"

"It was self-defence. He broke into my room and stole from me. So, I stabbed him. Sixty-nine times. It was to protect myself, protect the other patients."

"There's nobody in your room."

"What do you mean?"

"We've checked everywhere. Nobody has seen or heard anything from the ward, your room, and clinic."

"It definitely happened."

"Are you sure?"

"One thousand percent. He broke in and stole from me, then tried to kill me. I defended myself."

"Excuse me, I just need to speak with my colleagues."

He's walked out of the room again. I don't get what's left to understand. He's under those bin bags in the corner of my room. I'm one hundred percent, no, one thousand percent certain. I swear on my life. I never usually swear on lives, so that's really saying something. The doctor walks back into the naughty room with his head lowered. Like he's delivering me bad news. What's he going to tell me?

"There's nobody here. It's been over twenty-four hours."

These doctors are speaking out of their shitholes. Fine. If they don't help me sort out my problems, I'll have no choice but to do it myself.

"You know what, you're right, mate. I must just be, you know, must be mistaken."

"We'd like you to come for a full medical assessment."

"Fuck's sake. Do you not listen, you imbecile. That's right, I know the word imbecile. I don't need another medical examination. You can't make me come if I don't want to."

"I'm afraid you've got no choice."

"Touch me, and I'll overdose the next chance I get."

The doctor laughs and shrugs at me. He leaves, closing the door behind him. The handle comes loose and starts to dangle. The room isn't in good condition. I can hear a door down the hall slam closed. I can listen to many people, loud stomps making their way toward the naughty room.

My head starts to hurt. I can feel a pulsing sensation on both sides. I know what I need to do. I get down on my hands and knees. I crawl into the corner of the room. The footsteps get closer and closer. They're outside the naughty room. I see the dangling handle smash against the door.

"Who's there?"

No answer. They're here. Five of the big scary men in black walk over to me. I crouch down and back myself into a corner. Six-foot-six-inches towering over my slender five-foot-seven frame.

They all laugh at me.

"Laugh all you want, fucking pricks. All of you laughing. One after the other. What do you want from me? To make me dance and sing without my clothes on. It takes five of you barging your way into the naughty room. To do what? Drag me away for no reason. Or maybe worse. Maybe you'll all strip me naked and rape me over that broken, naughty stool. You all look like the type. I'll tell you it would take five of you right now. What terrible things will you do to me? Make it so that I can't stop crying. Screams. Blood. Thick jizz. Pointing at me. Recording me. Sending the photos and videos to everyone who works here, all your mates."

I wake up in my room all delirious. I must have passed out ages ago. There are puddles of sick next to me, all over my fucking face. I wipe the rank vomit from my cheeks and manage to stand up. I get out of bed and waddle over to the sink and pour myself a plastic cup of water.

I sway my way around my small and enclosed room. My heart has never beaten so fast in my life. A couple of boxes of my tablets are on the floor, next to a puddle of sick. I walk over to the tablets, grab them, and remove the packaging. I can't remember taking my daily dose. I'm pretty sure I usually take four. I pop four into my mush, one, two, three, four, and swallow with water.

I can already feel the difference. The clinic always used to tell me that more than two tablets would make me trip monkey balls. I eventually got the silly cunts to start letting me take four a day. I started taking two and built my way up to three. Before I knew it, I was taking four and freaking the fuck out. Now they just leave packets all over my room. As though they've just stopped caring if I overdose or not. They're probably sick of me speaking and just want me to shut the fuck up, to die in silence. That's when I feel most at peace. Lying in bed, eyes rolled back, tripping my nuts off, for hours and hours and hours. Not knowing what's real and what isn't. I'm still in stock of hundreds of these bloody tablets. I can't get through my day without them.

I put everything down on the table. Sway from side to side. I just about reach my bed, lie on my back, and look at the torn-apart ceiling. Turn onto the left side to avoid choking on my vomit and dying. I feel absolutely shattered. All of the other patients, shit, they're going to be so ashamed of me. I've let them down. Just like I've let everybody down. I'm so predictable. My eyes close, and I feel myself falling into a long, deep sleep.

I've not eaten in days. I'm absolutely starving. I've finally found a decent place to get some scran. The silly cow at the counter doesn't even respond. She just smiles and nods. Hopefully nipped off to rustle up my food. As I stand waiting, I see the blonde bird which served me, reasonably attractive, short with huge tits, speaking to what I assume is the manager. It might not be? But a name tag with 'Manager' helps clarify my assumptions. I step from one leg to the other, getting sick and tired of waiting. Where's my food? I cough loudly to get their attention. They snap their heads toward me, both looking and turning their backs. I can see them whispering and pointing. I'm not leaving until I've been fed. Every seat is taken. What the hell are they saying about me? I glance over to the seating area, and everybody's staring and whispering! There's an old dear, roughly eighty years old. She's got a walker to help her along the way. Her hands and feet are thick and swollen like watermelons. Looks like severe arthritis to me. One of the worst cases of disgusting inflammation I've ever seen. This ancient old goat is sitting next to her. He's got to be in his late eighties. Cauliflower ears. I doubt he can hear a bastard thing. Just nodding along to his wife, pointing toward me. I see an Asian couple sitting at the table behind them. They're talking about me in Arabic or one of their other non-English languages.

I seem to be the gossip point of the whole cafe. I see the blonde bird come over to the counter holding a sign. She slams the sign down in front of me onto the counter. She doesn't say a word. Just gives me evils and walks off. The sign reads in giant black letters, 'WE'RE CLOSED FOR BUSINESS.' I stand still. My mouth hanging open, arms by my side, hanging straight down, feet crossed, and legs tensed. My rosacea boots off and makes my face bright red. I look to my side, around the rest of the café. Everybody is leaving. They whisper under their breaths, cough in my direction, and scowl at me as though I've said or done something wrong. The old couple sighs as loudly as they can manage. The Asian couple calls me a cunt in Arabic or something. Every other group or couple shouts or hisses at me. I must loosen my body and keep guard in case they try to hit me. Luckily the only abuse I have to put up with is verbal. Although one kid, roughly fifteen years old, spits at my feet. I'm too shocked and scared to respond.

My hunger really kicks in. I'm starving to death! I need to eat. I start to feel dizzy. Dangerously anxious. Once everybody has left the cafe, blaming me and hating my existence, as they're forced out, I plan to defend myself against this ridiculous sign. I turn to the counter, and the staff has all left. It's just me. Alone. Whatever I've done has made them close down. They could have misinterpreted what I said? But that was merely land speak. We constantly mix up our words and play around with language. I guess I'm not eating here. I stroll out of the cafe, and theirs a sign that reads 'FOR SALE.' That sign definitely wasn't here when I arrived. For sale. Are they serious?

My presence and existence have made them sell the café? Surely not. I'm left wandering into a wilderness of confusion without explanation or reason, without a solid meal for three days. I knew that it was life or death. I needed to get a scran as soon as possible. I lightly stumble around and see the exact same signs on the front of every business. Cafes. Restaurants. Carts. Shops. All are completely closed down with for sale signs. Some are more specific than others. 'FOR SALE.' 'UP FOR SALE.' 'PLEASE BUY NOW.' Each establishment gets increasingly bizarre until I finally see something that makes sense. A giant photo of me! A digital image of me is on the massive screen for everybody to see.

I quickly bounce my way out of view before anything gets worse. As I scamper along, I pass through the busy masses. They all recognise me. They spit out words of abuse toward me. They confidently express their hatred for my existence. The groups scream and shout in my face until I'm forced to run, quicker and quicker, louder and louder. The mob grows, and I run faster and faster. I finally make it around a corner but quickly get spat at and hit in my nose. I continue to sprint further into the dark and grey streets. Finally, I lean against a wall and catch my breath. I stand there, taking deep breaths, dazed and confused, getting my bearings about me. Then, on the verge of tears, I collapse to the pavement, smashing my head on a drain pipe as I go down to the ground.

I attempt to sit up, but it's no good. I'm exhausted and weak. Absolutely no energy. I can see the cloudy and grey skies above. As my wooziness intensifies, I can't control a lethal fart, which rips out of my tight asshole and into the air. My stomach rumbles like a lion in a cage at the zoo. I try to control the rumbling but have no choice but to let another fart into the world. Another couple of farts squeeze their way out of my joggers. I shit myself. Lying on the cold, hard pavement, starving, unable to stand, I have no choice but to pump and trump as much as my body needs to. Diarrhoea dribbles out of my bum, down the back of my legs, and into the top of my socks. It smells like sewage and makes my eyes water. Not a single person attempts to help me. Some even walk over my body. A young kid runs over about seven or eight. He stands above my head and shouts at the top of his voice.

"Look! Look! He's shat his pants!"

Everybody bursts into fits of laughter. Then, they all gather around and kick me as I scream for help, but nobody comes.

"Fucking leave me alone!"
HAAAWWWHHH!!!
HAAAWWWHHH!!
HAAAWWWHHH!

CHAPTER 11

I run across the flat and trip over a loose floorboard, nearly standing on a nail sticking out. I begin to quickly and manically search across the room. I'm on my hands and knees, looking for any leftover bags of purple dust. Even just some tiny crumbs of cri-cringle-brekk. I check everywhere. Underneath the bath, my armchair, the floorboards. Nothing. Lass comes marching in. I pretend to be busier than I actually am so she doesn't think I'm some clingy boyfriend. She lightly pushes me to one side with her bare foot. Kicking my hand from under me. Using her dirty, blackened, long toenails, which dig into the back of my hand. The stench of her cheesy feet blows up my nose. I pinch the tip of my snout to get rid of the stink but end up ramming my fingers into both nostrils and tearing out the dried-up snot, which I wipe all over the floor. She flops back into my armchair and starts writing on her digital pocket pad. I flip her the middle finger, stand up and go back to drinking my whisky. Things haven't been the same the past couple of weeks. We argue all of the time. We never have sex. We never go outside. The only things we do together are shout, drink, cry, and sniff. I pretend her kick didn't affect me. I'm too busy. I'm the one who has attempted to tidy the gaff as best I could. I'm cleaning the flat to save our relationship.

"I'm sitting down because my legs are hurting, not because you ordered me to."

I lighten the mood by making the shape of a gun with my fingers. I'm feeling playful after my whisky. I slowly sneak up behind Lass. She's more focused on browsing through videos of girls piercing their bodies for a different currency. My fingers are more important than online tokens. I dive before Lass and pretend to fire my make-believe finger gun at her head.

"Bang! Bang!"

Lass looks up from her pad.

"What the fuck was that?"

I show Lass my gun fingers. They stink of beef, taste like shit and look like sausages.

"How old are you?"

"How old do you want me to be?"

"Act your age, not your shoe size."

"Come on, babe. Lighten up, and have a bit of fun."

"This is fun."

"When was the last time we just acted like kids?"

"You act like a kid daily."

"Alright then…well…when was the last time you just acted a like a kid?"

"Meaning what, exactly?"

"Letting go."

"Playing with kid's toys?"

I reload my finger gun, making clicking sounds with my mouth.

"I mean, just like, you know, acting a bit silly."

"Acting a bit silly?"

"Yeah."

"We act silly all the time."

"Sniffing cri-cringle-brekk doesn't count. Neither does killing people."

"Boring."

"Maybe boring to you, but to me, sniffing dust and slashing necks is getting boring."

Lass gets me told. Pulling the screen back to her face. I playfully dive out in front of her. She tries to avoid looking at me as I get ready to fire with my fingers.

"I swear down, fire that gun at me again, see what happens."

"Is that a threat?"

Lass looks up from her pad.

"Yeah, it is."

"Will you give me a spanking?"

"What's up with you?"

"I'm just saying, I can be a good boy, or bad boy, whichever you want."

"Is this you, flirting?"

"Maybe."

"It's pathetic."

"Why is it?"

"You're pointing fingers at me, pretending they're a gun."

"Let's have some fun, you boring bitch."

"Fun?"

"Yeah! Like the good old days. Let's drink, let's sniff, let's shag, let's kill, let's gossip, let's drink soup, let's get chased, let's hallucinate, let's masturbate, let's, let's, let's, let's fucking live life!"

I run around the flat and make shooting noises.

"Bang! Bang! Bang! Bang!"

I dive and fire the finger gun at Lass.

"Bang! Bang! Bang! Bang!"

"Right, that's it!"

Lass jumps up and chases me around the flat.

"Bet you can't catch me."

"I told you not to fucking start."

"Bang! Bang! Bang! Bang!"

Lass chases me in circles. She finally catches me, and we both wrestle like kids. We eventually reach the floor. Lass gets me in a headlock.

"Argh! You've got me, you win, you win, you win."

Lass releases me from her tight headlock. We both gasp for air with our legs crossed.

"That was fun."

"Yeah, it was."

I lean over to kiss Lass, but just as we're about to share a loving moment, she staggers onto her footsy-wootsy feet."

"What's wrong?"

"You're what's wrong. Dickhead. I told you not to shoot me, and you shot me twice, prick."

I stand up and move behind Lass. I try to comfort her.

"Fuck off."

"Alright, Jesus, I'm only playing about, trying to lighten the mood, have a bit of fun. We don't always have to be so serious."

"Maybe I want to be serious."

"This is why we should buy some purple, have a little sniffy-whiff."

"No. Now go play with your invisible toys."

"Fine."

Lass sits back in my armchair and returns to her ridiculous pad. I walk to my corner and have another whisky. Lass looks over at me disapprovingly.

"Here we go, he's drinking, yet again."

"I've tried to be myself. That's obviously not good enough for you."

"Loser."

"What the hell happened to you?"

"You happened to me."

I down my whisky. If she carries on like this, I'll spend every bit of credit we have on cri-cringle-brekk. Lass browses through her pad. I can hear animals getting household items shoved up their ass. I sit in silence, thinking deeply, having a drinky-winky.

"Stop being a bitch."

"I need to be a bitch, to deal with you."

"Deal with me?"

"Yeah."

"Meaning?"

"Mr Alcoholic, Mr Druggy, you're allowed to take one day off."

"I've had enough days off, thank you very much. Do you think that I want to be living like this?"

"Give it a rest."

"I've got no purpose, no reason to wake up in the morning, nothing to sober up for. Murder was fun. I loved it, that gave me some meaning, but you got bored too."

"Charming."

"The booze, the purple, it keeps me sane."

"Bollocks."

"It does."

"Sane from what?"

The whiskey has really kicked in. I'm starting to feel pissed like I could have a scrap or go downstairs and mug Teleport Boy for some sniff. I could drag Bog Roll into the flat and watch Lass drown her in the in the mouldy bath.

"Sane from this, from everything, this fucking, whole bleeding situation. I've lost my meaningful purpose."

Lass giggles and shrugs at me. She leans back in my armchair and distracts herself via the digital escape route.

"Moo! Moo!"

I hear animal videos.

"Oink! Oink!"

"Bitch."

"What?"

"Woof! Woof!"

Lass stops browsing the trending animal abuse videos.

We both go quiet. I walk around the flat, and Lass stays seated. We both silently reflect on the actual state of our relationship. Neither of us has said a word for a very long time. All we can hear are sounds off the street. Alarms. Abuse. Shouting. Screaming. Fighting. Fucking. Dealing. Dancing. Lass is buried in her pad. I'm gazing out of the hole in the window.

"Do you regret leaving?"

Lass blurts a question out of nowhere. She slowly puts down her pad and turns to me. I stand up and dawdle around the flat in circles, uncomfortable with her question. She is sure as hell choosing her moments.

"I know leaving was for the best. We couldn't have stayed any longer. I just regret how it happened."

I stare out of the hole in the window, looking up at the night sky. It's a full moon. Wow. It's truly unique. There's nothing like the night sky to remind you that we're all one thing. We can all see the same full moon. Whether you live on the land or in the city. We're all united. It's crazy how the sky can do that to you.

"You alright, babe?"

Lass has changed her tune.

"I always think about how things were left with the fam."

I'm not turning around to talk. It's so gorgeous up there. No wonder people want to live on Mars. I'm sure how things are going, Monsieur – long live the great Monsieur! – will manage to get us there. It will only cost us our souls.

"You needed to leave, babe."

"It's the way that it all happened."

I lean down and squint through the holes and cracks as much as possible. Lass comes over to me. I turn around as we come face to face.

"How would you describe going outside?"

Lass grabs the whisky from the floor. She has a few swigs, goes to the boarded-up windows, and looks out of the hole.

"What do you mean?"

Me and Lass are both in a state of deep reflection, thinking about the past.

"I've forgotten that feeling."

"Of going outside?"

"Yeah, like, how would you explain it."

"Pointless."

"Pointless?"

"There's no reason for anything. Everything's fallen apart, and no one's getting anything from anything. It's just there. Do you know what I mean?"

"No, not really."

"Everyone's just existing, trying to get by, trying to survive, rather than actually living. There's no meaning to any of it, to any of them. That's how I feel."

I lie on the cold hard floor and watch Lass as she gazes at the full moon.

"It was cloudy out there today, babe."

"Hmm."

"I don't mind it cloudy, sometimes."

"As long as it's not too cloudy."

"Cloudy can be good."

"Yeah, just not every single day."

"It's not cloudy every single day."

"Seems that way. I miss the blue sky"

"The blue sky's gone."

"How do we get it back?"

"We can't force the blue sky back."

"It's been mostly cloudy since we got here."

"Can't even remember the last time we had sun."

"Too long."

"It was always sunny when we were kids."

"Yeah."

"Days on the beach."

"Sunbathing."

"In the sea."

"Skinny dipping, late at night."

"Literally."

"It was like a summer's day for months, just me and you."

"I kept that love heart that you won for me."

"The teddy bear one?"

"Yeah."

"I meant it."

"Be mine forever."

"You were a big softy."

"Nah, not me."

"Remember our first kiss?"

"Yeah, only because you gave me a right hard on, stiff as a board, had to walk like a cripple."

"Nothing to do with me."

"But then it all stopped. You stopped it."

"It wasn't just me. You overreacted and drove me to it."

"We're here because of what you did."

"It was both of us."

"But you were the one who actually did it."

"I know!"

I jump up and pace around the contained space. I'm starting to sober up, and Lass has really hit a nerve.

"You didn't have to do it."

"I did have to do it."

This has always been a taboo subject, never to be mentioned again.

"You could have stopped yourself."

"I couldn't just leave you."

That was the rule, never to bring up what happened.

"You could have left me."

"It was my mess, it's still my mess, and it will always be my mess. So you didn't have to help me clean it up."

"I know deep down you didn't mean to do it."

"I fucking didn't, I fucking didn't, I fucking didn't. It was an accident."

"Exactly. Accidents happen."

"I fucking miss you. I wish you were still alive."

I face the door and feel like running outside. But I don't. I just think it.

"I know you do. Come here, babe."

"Nah, I'm alright."

I push Lass away from me and move back toward the window.

"I did what I had to do. It was self-defence. If anything, you all came at me first."

"No."

"I tried to leave."

"Hmm."

"They shouldn't have been so strict, you shouldn't have listened to them, they should have given us space to be who we wanted to be, you should have tried to see me, whatever the consequences."

"They were just trying to look out for you."

"No excuse. They knew we loved each other."

"We didn't deserve what you did."

"I needed love, not dosing up to the bastard eyeballs."

"Hmm."

"I know what you're trying to do."

"What's that?"

"Send me mad, with your digs, making me feel bad and hopeless, like there's nothing to even go outside for, well, I can't go out, alright. We agreed that was your job because I'd fuck things up and get us caught. So we agreed I'd stay here and look after this place."

"How's that going for you, babe? The place is a shit hole. Is this your attempt at looking after the place?"

"You clean it then, selfish bitch. At least I found it for us."

"Some dump, on a druggy estate, in a broken city,"

"Just shut up."

My neck tenses up, my shoulders are tight, my limbs go stiff, I need a piss, the room spins, I pace, I limp, I walk around the room. Lass pushes my buttons more and more.

She wants a fight, she wants a war, she wants a repeat of last time.

"It's not my fault. Probably all of that guilt."

"What do you want from me? Crazy, unstable, mental. That's me, right? Might as well live up to my reputation. I can't deal with you when you're like this. After everything I've done for you, you think I want to be here? You think I wanted to do what I did, to you, to them, to live in this shit hole, having to put up with you, put up with myself, my own mood swings, constantly, replaying it, repeating, so just shut up, shut it, for the love of God, shut the hell up."

"I'll leave. You won't have to put up with me. I'll go."

Lass rummages through her bag like a dying badger. She pulls her sleeping bag from the floor. She goes to pack her sleeping bag, but I aggressively snatch it from her. "I'll hand myself in."

"And, say what?"

"The truth."

"Nah, not the truth. You're all I've got."

"You're all I've got."

I hold Lass's hand, with her sleeping bag under my arm.

"I love you."

"I love you too."

"I should have stayed and faced what I did to you. The thought of you…lying there…lying at the bottom…bottom of the stairs…not moving."

"Hmm."

I let go of Lass's hand. I drop her sleeping bag, and we go to opposite ends of the room. She sits in my armchair, and I crawl into my corner.

"What do we do now?"

"Tell me, what do you want? I'm serious. Just tell me."

Lass asks me what I want to do. I think deeply about what I want.

"I want all of this to stop. I want to stop waking up every morning feeling scared. Like I'm about to be attacked or have a bomb blow up the gaff."

"A bomb?"

"Yeah, because that's how it feels. Every morning, I wake up scared, terrified that today will be the last. You know that feeling of something ending. Last time I laugh, last time I have a roof over my head, last time I see you, last time I'm free, last sniff, last drink. Fuck me sideways. I want to stop drinking. But I can't. If I could, I would have done it already. I can feel my insides rotting away, my liver's fucked, my heart's beating fast, my shit's turned black, my teeth are going yellow, and my skin is pasty. Drinking and drugs are killing me, but the only thing keeping me alive. It's my liquid oxygen. Keeping me sane. I want to stop being so insane and a nutter who kicks off and mouths off and gets so aggressive over nothing. I want to have dreams again and goals to work toward. I want to see you again if I can. I want to do something with my life. Fuck man, I want to leave this shit hole behind. I'm so done with all of this. Whatever's out there, whatever I'm actually running from, has got to be better than this. I want to bloody leave, I want to bloody leave, I want to bloody leave! I was wrong about us coming here because it was never going to last. Running away. How about we just face anything that's out there together, yeah? Face any consequences together."

Lass looks around the room. She quickly finds our shoes and hands over mine.

"I forgive you, babe."

"Lass?"

"Yeah?"

"Are we going outside?"

"If that's what you want?"

"More than anything."

"Let's do it."

"Promise?"

"Pinkie promise, a proper fucking promise."

"You're cute."

"You're cuter."
"You're funny."
"You're funnier."
"I'm scared. Are you?"
"Not anymore."
HAAAWWWHHH!!!
HAAAWWWHHH!!
HAAAWWWHHH!

CHAPTER 12

I slowly wake from a deep sleep and wriggle onto my left side. With only my right ear listening, I can hear the sound of tools smashing against the ground. I turn to lie on my back. Shooting pains trigger all throughout my body. The pain starts at my belly button, reaching both hips. A short sharp shock. Theirs's a firm knock on the door. I stare from my bed. I can't respond. I've forgotten how to speak. My tongue lifelessly rolls around in my mush as saliva dribbles onto my bedsheets. I've just been lying here. Moving around, even pissing in my bed. Sometimes even shitting myself. I'm always sick on my own chest.

"Are you awake?"

Argh! A lady's voice. I try to stay quiet and not make a sound.

"He's asleep."

She's not even seen me. How does she know if I'm asleep? She's clearly just a liar. I don't take too kindly to liars. I'm awake and lying on my back. The water-soaked ceiling looking all too familiar. I really want to let out a huge burp. If I can turn around onto my side, I can burp into my pillow, and this lady will leave me alone.

"How's he doing?"

I hear a bloke's voice. He's getting very close to the door.

"They're sending somebody soon."

I can't hold this burp in any longer. It's hurting my chest and giving me heartburn. I lean up and let out a viciously loud belch. I sound like a fog horn.

"Burgh!"

I hope those two mugs outside my room didn't hear me.

"Did you hear that?"

Oh shit! I'm guessing they heard me.

"He might be awake?"

Please don't come in, please don't come in, please don't come in, please don't come…A loud knock.

"Can we come in?"

I turn over, this time onto my right side, and let the left ear do all of the work.

"Let's just leave him alone."

"Argh!"

I shoot up as fast as I can.

"Argh!"

My body is in agony, and I begin to spaz out in pain, shooting, stabbing. These two fools barge into my room.

"Are you alright?"

"Argh!"

I had stabbing pains. Unbearable. They shot from my belly button into both hips. I finally get my bearings about me when this random fat woman, who I've never seen before, wearing a nurse's uniform, just sits at the foot of my bed and rubs my legs. I can't speak. It feels as though my tongue has swollen in my gob. This bloke, wearing a doctor's uniform, insists they leave me to it.

"It's alright. You don't have to say anything."

"Come on, let's just leave him alone."

That's right, listen to your colleague. Leave me the fuck alone. Instead, this fatty nurse comes toward me. The doctor bloke slowly walks her out of my room. I turn back onto my right side, away from these mugs. My eyes begin to water from the pain. The nurse and doctor soon leave, and they close the door behind them. I hear them down the hall. Tingles down my back. My lips begin to quiver. I take a deep breath.

I gaze over to the small table by my bedside. I see boxes and sachets. Tablets, drops, medicines, the complete works. I squint to make out the writing on my boxes. My eyes are too dry, and my vision is too fuzzy. I start to feel really sleepy. I have no choice but to close my eyes as I unavoidably fall asleep.

I wake up lying in a shit-stained pigsty, rolling around in my urine, in this crap hole of a room. It seems that I've shat and pissed my bed. My ass feels sloppy and squishy. A lot of the shit has crusted over my ass crack. My piss has soaked into the bed. It's stained through everything. The whole room stinks. I manage to sit up. I lean over to the small bedside table and grab some boxes of tablets. Half-empty boxes, so I must have been gobbling them like sweets. A half-empty cup of water is on the side, next to drops of medicine.

There's a light knock on the door. I simply grunt and make noises like a duck.

"Wack! Wack!"

That's all I've got to offer. Strange and weird animal noises.

"It's me. Can I come in?"

The door slowly opens. A surgeon waddles toward me and sits at the foot of my bed. She's wearing all of the surgeon gear, except she looks old as fuck.

"How are you feeling?"

I growl like a dog with rabies.

"It's alright. They're not coming in yet. It's only me."

The surgeon reassures me that it's just the two of us.

"This isn't easy for me, you know. It's the hardest thing that I've ever had to do. Taking young men, like you, some younger. But you don't care, obviously. Why should you? You're not going to remember it. I never once thought that things would turn out like this. This isn't how I imagined it. I took this job because I wanted to help people. I wanted to help young men. They've told us that we're doing this for you, for all the patients at the centre. Maybe we are. You boys deserve a lot more than this. More than this bed. More than the pain. Your life would have been terrible anyway. At least this is better than sitting in some cell for the rest of your life. You'll be better off somewhere else."

She walks toward the door and leaves. I'm alone.

I look at the ceiling and feel myself sitting on the golden sand. Waves crashing back and forth. The sun rising, the glorious view. I'm lying in a girl's arms, but I can't turn around to see what she looks like. We're looking out at sea, humming a song, almost like the waves slowly hitting the pier walls. I'm walking in the ocean. The water comes right up to my nose, just below the nostrils. I can smell the fresh air, taste the sea salt, and feel the big bright sun shining on my head. I can hear the sounds of the beautiful sea. They keep me calm.

I glance over at my medication. I look around at the other side of my room, and several technological devices are hooked together. Screens and lights are all tied up. One after the other, after the other, after the other. The digital world shines its glowing white light across the room. My head begins to tingle and hurt. I'm in too much agony to leave the bed. Seeing all those glowing technological fossils makes me cringe with pleasure and pain. I can't go on like this any longer. Swimming in rivers of my own piss. I'm ready for all of this brain rotting to end. My thoughts are sloppy, and my fantasies are mush. I manage to slowly close my eyes and quickly fall asleep.

The wind blows my chops backward, forcing my teeth to clench together. This helps me push through the pain. I manage to peek my eyelids open. I can see through the blistering highway mist. I move and puff through the cold. Slowly walking along the abandoned highway. I'm panting and gasping for air. But I'm still able to breathe. It feels as though I'm hiking up a steep mountain. The wind calms itself down. I hold onto a metal rail and rub the water from my eyes.

I can see the dark and empty night alone on a highway. I need to figure out where I'm heading. I need to find out where I'm allowed. I'm banned from everywhere. Maybe I'll be thrown off this highway. I plough my way forward. I've walked around for days wondering where I am. With very little memory other than the signs and symbols to indicate I'm not welcome. Every place, when they realise who I am, bans me from ever returning. They alert the rest of the towns and tell them that Lad is on the move. I leave before I'm chased. They chase me before I go. Each one completely closes down and packs up.

I pack up and leave. Leaving them to it. Who needs a place to sleep. Not me. Who needs food to eat. Not me. Who needs a drink. Not me. Who needs to travel. Not me. I can stay awake. I can eat leftovers out of bins and greenery from the forests. I can drink my piss or from rivers. I can walk. I can run. They have to keep an eye on thousands, just like me. I only have to watch them. I'm like a strategic general who will win out in the end. None of this bullshit about good winning over evil in the future. A load of bollocks. The most imaginative strategist always wins over the crying mobs. I see the light in the distance, which could mean anything. I push through the hardcore night-time breeze towards the bright and glowing symbol.

I reach the end of my highway walk, the unrecognisable light still off into the distance. I need to sit down somewhere. As nobody and nothing is around. I lie down on the pavement at the end of the road. If the mob finds out where I am, they will kill me. Nobody is a part of the mob by choice. But by force and bribery. They kill upon command and when demanded. They can kill their families, but I couldn't kill mine. I decided to flee. Wandering into the wilderness and dealing with the aftermath of mob events. I take in what's happened to me. Do I even exist without the acknowledgment of others? Am I a living being if I don't have the language ability? Fuck knows.

I can't tell if the bastard light is coming closer or getting further away. Perhaps both. Maybe the hunger and cold have kicked in, and the light doesn't even exist. I feel tired as the wind picks up again, faster and colder than before. Exhausted and hopeless, my eyes start to close, and my mush hangs open. I slowly allow my hunger to make me see things that aren't really there. I lifelessly roll onto my side with my blinkers closed and gob open. Feeling myself drift into sleep. I lie there for a while, freezing my tits off and waiting to evaporate into the late winter dust. Before feeling my last breath, I hear a female voice. The voice gets closer and closer, louder and louder, lighter and lighter. A girl's face. We are both smiling at each other. I can tell she cares about me.

"I forgive you, babe. Think of the blue skies and crashing waves."

I eventually wake up from my long sleep. Still in the same bed, drowning in piss and shit. Two completely different doctors walk in. They're both wearing white lab coats and masks. An attractive Asian female and a speccy ginger nerd.

"Hi there. Can you just lie down for us, please?"

Politely asks the stunning Asian beauty.

I nod and put my feet up, lying flat on the bed.

Both pull out a tray of equipment. I lean over and see what they're working with. There are syringes that they're filling up.

"You can relax. This won't take long."

Insists the speccy ginger geek.

"You're doing really well. It won't hurt."

Assures the stunning Asian beauty.

"You won't feel a thing."

I'm not the brightest spark in the box, but I know exactly what's happening.

I always thought I'd cry or be shocked when my moment came. But, instead, I know that my ride is up and my time is here. To be fair to him, the speccy ginger nerd holds my left arm gently.

"You're doing really well. This will all be over before you know it. I promise it won't take long."

The stunning Asian beauty loads the syringe. I close my eyes. I'm aware these are my final thoughts before I die. I quickly try to think of what I want my last thoughts to be. How do I summarise this experience? If I can. I don't remember much. But I can feel a lot. I feel a sense of gratitude that I'm even here. I squeeze the bed sheets with my right arm to ease the pain as she slowly inserts the needle into a vein in my left arm. The stunning Asian beauty unloads liquid into the vein as I close my eyes. I'm grateful to have had the opportunity to have been here.

"Thank you."

End

Ingram Content Group UK Ltd.
Milton Keynes UK
UKHW040650070423
419815UK00004B/224

9 781399 950572